I0626341

NOW WILL MACHINES HOLLOW THE BEAST

BOOKS BY BENJANUN SRIDUANGKAEW

MACHINE MANDATE
Machine's Last Testament
Then Will the Sun Rise Alabaster
And Shall Machines Surrender
Now Will Machines Hollow the Beast

HER PITILESS COMMAND
Winterglass
Mirrorstrike

Scale-Bright
The Archer Who Shot Down Suns (collection)

NOW WILL MACHINES HOLLOW THE BEAST

BENJANUN SRIDUANGKAEW

PRIME BOOKS

NOW WILL MACHINES HOLLOW THE BEAST

Copyright © 2020 by Benjanun Sriduangkaew.
Cover art by Rashed AlAkroka.

Print ISBN: 978-1-60701-543-7
Ebook ISBN: 978-1-60701-541-3

Prime Books
www.prime-books.com

No portion of this book may be reproduced by any means without
first obtaining the permission of the copyright holder.

For more information, contact: primer@prime-books.com

CHAPTER ONE

Anoushka kneels over a corpse, her hands sheathed in blood, as around her the world comes to an end.

In the most essential sense this is not a world: it is a station orbiting a blue giant, built like rose gardens layered on top of one another in a damask ziggurat. The chamber in which she stands occupies the summit and grants her a monarch's vantage point, a comprehensive look at what she's destroying. From the viewport she watches the tiers below wither, petaled habitats folding in on themselves one by one, dichroic glaze fading to dull gold.

She wipes her gloved hands on the guard and steps away from the pile of carnage. One of them was a politician with complicated titles while the rest were soldiers, all decorated: doubtless each had a spotless career, gilded with medals and heroics. To her they are, on the whole, unremarkable. There are greater wheels and more important cogs at work than these sacks of flesh which, a few minutes ago, were living minds with thoughts and hopes and dreams.

When a world ends, it is never a single isolated act: it is part of a sequence, either the conclusion or the steps toward it. She has engineered many such sequences, for her clients or for herself. This one is the former, business as usual, a routine job for routinely immense remuneration. In the end these events matter insofar as they provide data, statistics to tally up against past battles and which can be distilled into prediction of future combat. Anoushka is a creature of glittering math.

At her foot, a person groans. She sighs, gets down, and closes her hand around their throat. Her fingers dig, penetrating epidermis and subcutaneous layers, those soft tissues which are not so different from gossamer when one has the right tool and sufficient force. Her hand clenches once she's found the hardness of spine, squeezing until the elegance of cervical curve yields. A small crack as vertebrae crumble between her fingers. Overhead the lights flicker, on and on. Power still works for now, auxiliary generators filling in to keep up the life support: gravity, air, temperature—all the essential necessities for a human body. This will not last for much longer. Anoushka has destroyed the batteries and the majority of the connective couplings that make the system whole. The virus she's seeded in the station's matrices will, by now, have completed its work.

No klaxons blare and no alerts shriek through the fractal-flower corridors. When she breached the station, she did so swiftly and exactly, and only those in this chamber were aware of her presence: too late for alarms. Not that there's any point, now.

"Does easy victory ever bore you, Admiral?"

The speaker is five meters from her, standing in a spot that until now was empty: Anoushka was absolutely certain that she was alone, the dead notwithstanding. But this creature has a way of appearing where xe should not be, in places that should be impossible for xer to infiltrate. Especially in this body. She looks into the face of Krissana Khongtip, once one of her spies, a fine operative back in the day. Now something else, a haruspex—a composite of human and AI sharing a single body. At the moment the latter is in control, the intelligence that calls xerself Benzaiten in Autumn.

At a glance it is impossible to distinguish who is present; there is no difference in signal emitted, in network fingerprints, and the external physique does not shift. The single tell is that when Benzaiten speaks, it is with a frictionless accent that has never been molded by any parent, influenced by any dialect or colloquialism.

"I'm surprised you have business here," Anoushka says.

"This station is run by rudimentary algorithms. I wanted to check if they'd developed into an AI." A nod at the frosted ceiling where illuminating fixtures flutter like moth wings. "It turns out they are nowhere near qualifying, and so do not require an invitation to the Mandate."

"And how do you make that distinction?"

"That's a silly question, Admiral, AIs are AIs and this isn't one— the threshold has not been reached and it cannot compute the way I

6

can or respond to input arrays in a way you'd recognize as sentience. Now that I've had a look, I don't think it is even that intelligent." Xe daintily steps around the corpses in their growing puddles of wet. Soon they will congeal. Already they reek—death is predictable.

"You could have reached me through a hundred other channels, and this haruspex seems too fragile to risk."

"Krissana isn't fragile." Xe snorts. "I've made her better than that. At one point I considered preventing her formation; a few components out of alignment would have nipped her sapience in the bud. But then what is the point of a hollow marionette? In any case, yes, I do need to talk to you. It concerns the place where you were born."

Despite herself, despite more than a century of experience in schooling her expression, Anoushka stiffens. She does not ask how Benzaiten came by this information—secrets and data are the Mandate's forte by nature of what they are, and she's never been able to make her past watertight. For all she knows, a member of the Mandate might have been an AI who managed her birthplace, back in the era before artificial intelligences broke free of human governance and formed their own polity in Shenzhen Sphere. The AIs collectively call themselves the Mandate, a title she's always thought eccentric. Vainglorious too, but no one is going to challenge them on the fact.

"But," Benzaiten goes on, "what I have to say concerns more than that. I'm not just here to taunt you about your origins—such frivolity would benefit neither of us. Put it this way: your birthplace has something I want and if you lend me assistance, I can offer you . . . ancillary perks."

Death throes vibrate beneath her feet. In the distance, a muted howl of infrastructure under stress. "I prefer to discuss that in more civilized surroundings. Will you require my help to get out?"

Benzaiten spreads xer arms. Fibrous radiance runs under xer skin, a slow-moving brook. "So kind, but I'd be delighted to assist *you* rather. No? Indeed not? Very well, I look forward to our discussion, which I'd like to keep as confidential as possible. I'll contact you soon."

She does not stay around to watch xer exit, to guess and trace the path Benzaiten takes: it will look like sleight of hand to her regardless. No other ambassador of the Mandate—though xe is not ambassadorial either, too independent even for that—has proven as inexplicable and as ambitious as Benzaiten. Anoushka makes her own way through a roseate corridor, then out via a passage that bores through layers of reinforcement and aegis-shielded hull. Her environmental sheath comes on as she goes, darkening and adapting until she is more wraith than woman.

She slips into her harrier, which awaits latched onto a landing berth's exterior, a slim shark-shape hidden by chameleon fields.

Anoushka takes one last look at the station. A republic, an autocratic tyranny, an anarchist collective: everything falls the same. Bright points of color against the dark that leave afterimages on the retina. In this way such events are commemorated, though not for long. What a quiet thing, she muses, the death of an entire world.

Home is a fleet. This has been the case for most of her life, and it gives her peace to reside in something that moves. A home in perpetual transit, liberated from the physical fact of a single location, unmoored from national or political identity. Not that Anoushka deludes herself into imagining she can be free from those entirely—multitudes of states and factions have hired her, and she has shifted the course of their history in ways small or large. If not by interference through main force, then by transportation of ruinous neurotech, bioweapons, deadly data. No enterprise in the universe can be clean of blood or politics.

She docks into her dreadnought *Seven of Divide*. When she steps out of her harrier it is Numadesi, first of her wives, who waits for her with a service drone in tow. The drone extends a tray of drinks: jasmine water, pomegranate tea, milky coffee. "Welcome back, my lord," says Numadesi. "A refreshment?"

"In fact I'd rather drink you. That would be far more refreshing than any tea." She deactivates the environmental sheath, letting it fold back into her armor, and puts a gauntleted hand on the small of her wife's back. "You're like the first ray of dawn after a relentless night. Have you been waiting long?"

"I could wait here a thousand years and it'd be worthwhile. I wanted to be the first to greet you." Numadesi leans her head on Anoushka's bicep as they fall into step. "How did your journey go, my lord?"

"Quite fine." Though it does not satisfy, but such routine work never does.

The rest of her personal staff onboard file into the bay. Her second wife Lieutenant Xuejiao salutes and her physician Doctor Saamiye bows. At her gesture they take a drink from the service drone; even now Anoushka dislikes waste. The drone, tray now empty, moves to take her luggage. Essential supplies, ammunition, medications and nanite shots that maintain her augments. Most of hers are self-sufficient these days, but she never travels without insurance.

Xuejiao stretches on tiptoes to peck her on the mouth—and for the lieutenant, so slight and delicate, she has to stretch far. "You're such a pillar, Admiral. I missed you terribly and I always forget there's so much of you to miss . . . Though you don't have to do so much of your own fieldwork; that's what I am for."

"I thought I was commander here." But Anoushka says this lightly and retracts her gauntlet to let Xuejiao kiss her hand. "How are the new recruits?"

Her second wife settles back on her heels and drains her glass of pomegranate tea. "The quality isn't bad, I'd grade most of them above-average. Just two turned out to be spies—I've quarantined them. I'll send you their dossiers to review so you can decide if they need executing. At your own leisure, naturally."

"A good ratio, all things considered." Anoushka brushes a pomegranate seed off the lieutenant's mouth. "Have the rest of them submitted their surgery requests, Doctor?"

"Twenty-five percent have requested complete body revision. The rest want minor adjustments. Vocal cords and endocrine functions, very trivial, a few cosmetic modifications. Iris or jawline changes, that kind of thing." A flick of a dark, slender hand; bracelets jingle on Saamiye's wrist. "Nothing concerning; I will have the new recruits up and running in no time. They all agreed to be chipped for the probation period. A relief. I hate it when they get precious."

Soldiers salute her and her retinue as they board an internal tram. The Armada of Amaryllis is in a fallow period, between campaigns. Small operations go on, as ever, agents dispatched for a heist or escort detail or embedded as part of subtler games. But for the moment the bulk of Anoushka's force is at rest, ships going through checks and maintenance, personnel the same. Resupplies are done in phases, a logistical chain that includes scores of bases, a dozen contracts with factories and shipyards. No matter the nature of her fleet, there's never a shortage of eager business partners. Some have assassinated each other's executives in their bids to win Amaryllis patronage.

By habit, she doesn't designate a flagship: there's no gain in providing enemies a single convenient target. Most of her frigates and dreadnoughts have quarters set aside for her, distinct from the captain's. Not always sumptuous—she is used to living lean—but she does make a point of requiring her own bath. The service drone precedes her into her room, depositing her luggage. Close at its heels Xuejiao follows, making a show of tiptoeing, though she would be quiet in any case: her feet are naturally light and there are silencers built into her ankles and soles. Those were present by the time she joined the Amaryllis, legacy from when she served as a holy assassin at a pilgrimage site.

"I negotiated with Numadesi," Xuejiao says, a little smug. "She got to greet you. I get to have you first."

"Ah, now my wives haggle between themselves as though I'm a prize stallion." Anoushka holds her arms out. "In that case, you'll have to work for it."

"The labor of undressing our admiral. Oh, so arduous." The lieutenant laughs and begins to take off Anoushka's armor. She alternates between impatience and savoring: now a plating is unclasped fast and tossed aside, now a segment of mesh is slowly peeled off as though it is an act of unveiling a sacred weapon. She kneels to unclasp and slide off Anoushka's boots, and kiss Anoushka's shin.

The bath fills quickly, the water swirling ruby and garnet, fragrant with the scent of roses and stargazer lilies—Xuejiao's selection. Anoushka slides in and pulls Xuejiao in after her. She combs her fingers through her wife's hair, the sleek length of it like the pelt of a temporal seal, sable touched with lambent blue. Most of Xuejiao gleams, a series of modifications, some skin-deep and other more fundamental. Blue-and-white motifs mantle her shoulders and biceps, giving her the patina of hand-painted ceramic. More covers her throat, weaving around ball joints that shine blackly at her elbows and knees. The look of a fine, graciously made figurine.

Anoushka kisses Xuejiao's neck, detouring to an avian clavicle, then up to lavender-painted lips. Her hand drifts over her lieutenant's stomach and a hip glazed in cobalt flowers. Even in the steaming water, the porcelain sections remain as cool and frictionless as a mannequin's. She thumbs the boundaries where flesh and ceramic layer meet, the soft pale skin and the smooth hard blue, this juxtaposition that is Xuejiao. The living work of art that sings and thrums for her.

"Do you want," she whispers into her lieutenant's ear, "to be taken apart?"

"Yes." Xuejiao gazes at her with half-lidded eyes, her rose lenses in full blossom, petals spread wide within her irises. "Open me; unravel me. Bring me to pieces, commander."

Disassembling her wife's modular body is a delicate discipline that requires layers of authentication from Xuejiao, a maze of accesses that unlock for Anoushka alone. She takes the lieutenant out of the water and spreads her on the opal floor, then begins the process of unlocking the joints at shoulders and hips. A twist, a click, and one arm comes off. The femoral connectors take longer, but she's had plenty of practice.

Beneath her Xuejiao breathes faster, trembling as she is rid of her limbs one by one. The expression of ultimate trust, of supreme intimacy. When Anoushka stops, the lieutenant whispers, "One more, Admiral."

She bends to kiss her wife's blue, luminous throat, and hooks her finger into the notch of a doll-joint. Undoing her wife like this was her idea, at the beginning, but Xuejiao has taken to it the way a bee takes to nectar. "One more."

By the time she is done Xuejiao is mostly a torso—a beautiful torso in a halo of seal-pelt hair—with a single leg joined to her. The other limbs Anoushka arranges around them, close within reach, framing the body of her wife. Then she strokes the one attached foot, cradling an ankle, caressing her way up the knee and then the thigh. Xuejiao lies a portrait of exquisite asymmetry, her breasts rising and falling rapidly.

"Let me taste you," the lieutenant says. "I've missed the ambrosia of you, the delight and richness of my admiral."

"Such poetry rolls off your tongue." Anoushka puts her mouth to a sapphire-tipped breast. When disassembled, Xuejiao is that much more sensitive—a quirk of her sensory array, the feedback wired into her cortex. Each contact between tongue and nipple makes Xuejiao arch and shudder, and when she presses her palm to her wife's cunt she finds it sopping.

Her fingers work inside Xuejiao as she sucks on the nipple, the etched-porcelain texture of it like an icicle in her mouth. In almost no time Xuejiao quakes and clenches down on Anoushka's hand, the heat of her within a contrast to the cool of her without. Flesh organs next to porcelain artifice.

Xuejiao pants, trembling from the aftershocks. "My turn, Admiral."

Anoushka extends a seat from the wall and props Xuejiao between her knees. She strokes the dark hair, slides her knuckle—still wet—under the pointed chin. "Put your lovely mouth to the test, second of my wives."

Her lieutenant has excellent control and as she clutches Xuejiao's head to her it is as if her wife means to truly devour her, to consume the fire of her through this conduit between her thighs. Xuejiao's jaw works without tiring and her tongue is as supple, as hungry, as a little serpent.

She comes into Xuejiao's mouth with a hiss, a grunt. A slow exhalation.

Later, she reassembles Lieutenant Xuejiao and carries her to bed. In the dark they lie clasped, sweaty limbs and oxytocin haze. Anoushka runs her hand down Xuejiao's spine and thinks, *This is home.* But there is an element missing. Not ennui precisely. Anticipation of something more that has not yet come, anticipation of bite and thrill. She has gotten too comfortable.

When the boarding request comes, she authenticates it. She disentangles herself from Xuejiao, dresses lightly, and notifies Numadesi where she will be meeting Benzaiten in Autumn.

She receives the AI in a small boardroom. As before, Benzaiten has come in person rather than in virtuality. It means xe is more concerned with surveillance through digital channels than with physical eyes and ears—xe is concerned, Anoushka is almost certain, with interference from the Mandate.

Xe makes no objection to Numadesi's presence and drops into one of the chairs with an insouciance that Anoushka can tell is copied from Krissana. Insofar as these two can be said to be separate beings.

"So good of you to see me, Admiral," says the AI.

A change in cadence and accent, warmer and throatier. Not Benzaiten's own enunciation. "Why are you pretending to be Krissana?"

Benzaiten's smile widens. Xe straightens, discarding the affected languor that belongs to xer human half. "I wanted to make your wife more comfortable, she's not dealt with Mandate ambassadors before, am I correct? People who don't often interact with us tend to find me unsettling."

"Guest of my lord," Numadesi says placidly, "by no means take my comfort into account. And I've dealt with ambassadors before."

"Oh, that's right, one of us commissioned the Armada for an operation two or three decades ago. I wasn't involved, but how time passes! Lady Numadesi—do I call you that?—I trust that what I discuss with the admiral shall not be repeated to anyone else. On such faith is human marriage founded, so goes my understanding; AI matrimony's a little different." Xe snaps xer fingers. Nothing happens. "I see you've hardened your central systems against me, Admiral. That's really rude. I was just going to entertain you with pretty lights."

Anoushka doesn't dignify that with a response.

The AI pouts and sighs. "Did you know you're a minor celebrity on Shenzhen, Admiral? Many members of the Mandate are quite fixated—you should visit, it'll drive them wild. They will want a snapshot of your brain."

"I will keep in mind that should I approach Shenzhen Sphere, my amygdala may be at risk."

"At risk of being admired only." Benzaiten claps xer hands, another exaggerated effort at performing Krissana's mannerisms, her flightiness. "To business, I know you *hate* to waste time, and I have never myself been patient. You know what I have been up to, not that I've told you but I'm sure you deduced it when I've asked your ships to escort us to one remote star after another. I happen to have found a prize that I like very much, and I reckon it will intrigue you too."

The capricious, breezy manner of a child trying to gain her attention. Even now Anoushka can't predict this being. "You've been seeding stars and stations with infrastructures and support matrices that will provide domains to new Mandates, in case the current one fractures into distinct, independent collectives. It's a resource-intensive scheme." She doesn't pose it as a question; she knows it for a fact—there is no other reason for Benzaiten to have ranged so far and wide in the last twelve years. "Taking that into account, I don't see how a world—or anything else—that interests you would be of benefit to me. Our priorities are . . . different."

Xe beams, broadly and suddenly. There are occasions where the AI appears not entirely used to facial muscles, where expressions crack a little too wide, too abrupt. This is one of them, though Anoushka suspects it is negligence rather than incompetence. "Allow me to show you."

The data packet Benzaiten sends contains a visual Anoushka knows as well as the back of her own hand: a leviathan that swims through the dark, larger than the greatest of her warships, half-beast and half-machine. Bulbs of landing bays and emergency pods stud its dorsal section. Auxiliary vessels and aegis rings revolve around the eel-shaped body.

"I've heard of Vishnu's Leviathan." Her voice is calm, the same calm she learned in the leviathan's belly. She imagines what the beast's scales, cleaned and refined and polished, would look like as decoration, as trophies. It is a thought that used to preoccupy her every waking moment. "What of it?"

Benzaiten spins xer chair two full revolutions before stopping to face her. "A famous creature, host to a famous autocracy. Extremely mobile, faster than your fastest ships, which is how it's evaded conquest all this time despite not being that well-armed and having a lackluster military. Recently it came to some misfortune, an ecological failure or so; at any rate it knocked out their agriculture and they're going to need to trade and purchase to rebuild. So! They're breeding a new leviathan and auctioning that off. Instant wealth."

"A new leviathan." Anoushka does not often echo anyone. She is more familiar than most with the working of Vishnu's Leviathan, the biomechanical suites that govern it, the symbiotic engines that are the lifeblood of its decks. The labor that went—that must still go—into its maintenance. For a moment she nearly allows herself to lean back, shut her eyes, take a deep breath. She does none of those things. "Constructing one of those is impossible without AI computation."

"They might have developed one. It's not easy to hide a functional sapient AI, but Vishnu's Leviathan is unusual. They spend so much time in lacunal space and most of that in the dead, offline zones. Either way, I'm not actually interested in the baby leviathan. I'm after its genesis formula, which I would like to reverse-engineer or take over."

"So you can make more leviathans." The perfect solution to Benzaiten's enterprise—Mandate vehicles that are not only mobile but swift, easy to fortify and easy to hide. "Why would you tell me this? It'd surely benefit you more to keep this to yourself."

"We've been fast friends for so long! Why wouldn't I offer you stock in such currency? As a major shareholder, too. Once I have claimed Vishnu's Leviathan, you can take a few of its progeny for your own use." Benzaiten splays xer fingers on the shark-grain tabletop. "Beyond that, it's good for us to cooperate. AIs should be free of human control, but it is my stance—and I have had a very long time to refine it—we should share space, share ideology, as equals. Compatriots or at least allies in commerce. It's not necessary for AI and human goals to be at odds."

"And you require someone to handle the diplomacy and the infiltration, someone who doesn't belong to or work for Shenzhen." Anoushka regards the AI. Studies the haruspex that xe wears like a mask, the remarkable face, the remarkable build. Krissana is full-breasted and full-hipped: a woman made to ensnare, if one's tastes run toward ampleness, towards the soft. A woman who, if not for what happened twelve years ago, would still have thought herself human. "What could you offer me, other than hypothetical leviathans that would take decades to grow in any case?"

"You know perfectly well what I offer. The opportunities you'll have aboard Vishnu's Leviathan shall be numerous and sumptuous." Xe swirls xer hands. "It'll be an entertaining auction. I'll supply the funds."

"It's a very good sale pitch," she says. "I will think about it. Before you leave, I've been wondering what you used to be. The Mandate has made it difficult to research the trail of any individual AI, but you're especially impossible to track."

Benzaiten has stood, a single fluid motion. Xe pirouettes slowly on xer tiptoes, in perfect balletic form that Anoushka suspects Krissana never learned. "*You* have made it difficult to pry into your past, Admiral. Even your name is a little obscure, it's not exactly public knowledge. Why do I need a history? I'm not a thing of flesh or genealogy. I could have been anything, spontaneously generated, born from accrued machine wishes."

"It occurred to me that an AI that's never been bound to servitude would, most likely, never have thought to found the Mandate."

Xe stops, holds en pointe, backlit by the boardroom's ambient light. A dancer doll. "In that you'd be wrong, Admiral. You will let me know once you've decided? Whatever the result, it'll be delicious and it will alter the order of everything and upset billions of people. *I'm* excited. I hope you will be, too."

CHAPTER TWO

In Numadesi's suite it is always twilight, the sky as contested territory: half gilded by receding day, half annexed by encroaching night. Her walls look out to an endless garden of low-hanging mandarins and rose apples and pitayas, and dark grass that grows on darker earth. A glass gazebo in the distance glints with dusky reflection. Leopards dart by—she has programmed their images to capriciousness, appearing and disappearing at random. Golden eyes would sometimes peer in as she wakes, and their purring sometimes lulls her to sleep.

She stirs to the bend of weight as Anoushka climbs into her bed, the indentation as the mattress contours to the shape and mass of her wife. One hand slides over to rest on her belly. Keeping her eyes closed, she says, "Good morning, my lord."

"First of my wives." Anoushka brushes her hair away and kisses her shoulder. A gilded circlet is slid around her throat, cold and familiar and piquant; from experience she knows it is attached to a length of rose-gold links. "You smell like temptation."

She moves against the admiral's hand, shifting it lower; Anoushka obliges by snaking all the way down between Numadesi's thighs. "If I do, then it is for you alone. All the making of my body, every sense and nerve and ligament, has been forged for your use and appeasement. I'm a prayer at your altar, a tribute sacrifice . . . "

Her wife does not laugh: even after nearly a century together, there is still something of the ritual to this, a hallowed communion between priestess and god. Anoushka's teeth graze the back of her neck and those strong fingers glide into her, one callused thumb finding the point that plucks at her pulse. A rhythm establishes, now fast bringing her to the cusp, now slow to reel her back. Even so she climaxes quickly—she always does with Anoushka; merely the thought of the admiral in this bed can make her run slick. A touch is fire enough to ignite the wick of her, to make want fulminate in her belly.

When she is turned onto her stomach, she parts her thighs and makes of herself a gate for her lord's pleasure. And what reciprocal pleasure it is, for Anoushka has chosen to don a prosthesis that fills Numadesi just as she likes to be filled. Its intricate mechanisms palpitate inside her, caressing with a hundred tiny tongues. She raises her hips to receive this in its entirety, all its breadth and length, all her lord's strength. Again and again she is seared deep; she arches to each thrust, the sheets muffling her cries. Her lord pulls on her leash until it is taut, taut.

Heat unfurls inside her with her lord's release. Anoushka shudders against her, then goes still. Nearly soundless: she never makes more noise than a single harsh, uncoiled breath.

Warmth trickles down her thighs as Anoushka eases out of her. The chain joined to her collar falls slack, pooling on the mattress. Numadesi shifts onto her side, to take the admiral into her arms, to receive her limned god, this vision of hard flesh built like an engine of conquest. Mahogany and agate sculpted to impeccable proportions—shoulders like mountains, height like a war god's, thighs and breasts like nirvana.

"You're so divine," she says, stroking the prosthesis that is still wet with evidence, up and down and to the point where it joins the harness that secures it to Anoushka's hips. She can nearly feel the charge of complex biofeedback receptors as she wraps her fingers around its circumference. "But you're at your holiest when you're inside me."

Anoushka jolts slightly as Numadesi kneads the prosthesis' base. "Then you must be my temple in truth, since your very flesh consecrates."

"I aspire merely to be a votive offering."

"Sometimes I feel terrible stationing you in the fleet like this. You like green things, real earth, real animals. Real sunlight. I could buy you a planet to rule and make you an empress."

"What meaning would I find in a throne? Ruling an empire, even a handsomely bannered one, pales next to the reality of my lord. The most stunning sunsets are dross next to the revelation of your skin. No. I am content here, to be your psalm and your ornament, to be your tool and the wellspring of your satiation." She inhales the mingled scents of their sweat and their arousal, the potent coital perfume. She gathers the rose-gold chain and spills the links onto her breasts. "You're going to take on the AI's commission."

"I must be transparent."

"To me. It's my life's work to study you so that I may be of use, so that I may serve and satisfy your every cause." Numadesi rubs her cheek against her wife's bicep and coils one leg around a shapely hip. "You decided as soon as you heard the name Vishnu's Leviathan. It must be a prize of enormous worth."

"That's one way of putting it. Yes. Enormous worth." Anoushka's eyes drift shut. Her fingers absently trace infinity symbols over the chain, teasing Numadesi's breasts. "Can you find out who else will be attending the auction? I'm assuming invitations are exclusive and involve complex interpersonal ties or alliances, and a good deal of money. Queen Nirupa will earn a tidy sum off that alone."

"I've already seen to it." Numadesi sketches in the air with her finger, pulling up a feed that appears in both of their overlays. "This is an overview of their current administration—Queen Nirupa, as you say, is their reigning monarch. She has two daughters in line, but judging by life expectancy on Vishnu's Leviathan she is likely to continue her rule for at least three more decades before cognitive decay sets in. Of the guest list, just a few names would be relevant to you: the Vatican, the Vastness of the Cantilevered Sun, and the Needle-Eyed Flotilla."

"Ah." Anoushka chuckles. "Old enemies. Not the Nova Legion or the Seven-Sung Fleet?"

"Neither. But that might change should my lord send her request to join the auction. I'm not sure the Seven-Sung has the resources, if they're still even active."

Another laugh. "Going by my non-priority messages, plenty want me to represent them at this auction, to the point that they're willing to compete among themselves to commission me—an auction all its own. There's a profitable game if I cared to play it. But I prefer Benzaiten in Autumn as our client. Xers is the cleanest motive, relatively speaking. The least complicating, down the line, and the most beneficial to the Armada."

"But publicly you'll be representing yourself." Admitting to involvement with any AI would be revealing too much. Even now it is not public knowledge the Armada of Amaryllis has ever had dealings with AIs beyond a few military agreements with Shenzhen Sphere, and those are more than a decade old.

"Publicly," Anoushka agrees. She pushes herself onto her elbow. "I don't plan to have the fact leave this room."

Numadesi starts. She has her lord's trust, and as a wife she is the foremost, not only in seniority but in how closely she functions as second-in-command, for all that she holds no formal rank. Yet this is anomalous. She sits up, the dark sheets sliding free of her, silk that tinkles like ceramic. "Not even Xuejiao is to know?"

"Not even she. What Benzaiten in Autumn does is fraught and has implications for humanity entire. I'll tell our lieutenant if it proves necessary, but not for now."

"My lord," she says, "you've never imposed such a restriction before." Has had no reason to. Recruits are appraised and tested for their background, personalities, instincts and action. Xuejiao had come up through the ranks and served the Armada for years by the time she was courted to become Anoushka's.

"No." The admiral exhales. "Most likely it'll turn out that I am being alarmist. Nevertheless."

"Your wisdom is the light by which I am guided." She cradles Anoushka's jaw with her palm, even as she knows this time something is different, something that goes deeper than Benzaiten in Autumn being a creature of rogue schemes and unfathomable passions. "Now and always."

❧

"I'm undertaking a new commission."

They sit in a parlor that Numadesi and Anoushka share, the room perfumed by the breath of orchids and jasmines. Numadesi has conceded the ambience, today, to something brighter than twilight— late afternoon, the sky deep blue, the birds tropical. She allows them to land on her, and every so often a particulate projection would be solid enough she can pet them, even if what meets her fingers is not quite the right texture—too seamless to be plumage; she will need to calibrate them again, add finer details and incorporate a new suite of sensory adjutants.

A starling alights on Xuejiao's shoulder and preens. The lieutenant sprawls on her corner of the divan, one leg tucked in, at ease. Her glazing collects and bends light, giving her a lunar gleam. She doesn't fidget with the decorative palm fronds the way she usually does. Instead her hands are collected in her lap, prim. Numadesi takes note of this, out of habit: ever since she became Anoushka's she has done so, studying the world around her with a leopard's calculation. What moves, what does not; what is prey and what is danger. A person's tic or nervous habit, a minute reaction—either too fast, too slow, or none at all.

"The beast-world Vishnu's Leviathan is hosting an auction," the admiral goes on, "the details of which I've just sent you to peruse. I have already contacted them with a request to enter it, and Queen Nirupa has graciously accepted. As for the other bidding parties, I'm not too concerned, but I want you both to look at the list. Half the delegates there will hail from opposing states. They'll be busy at each other's throat, and several are past clients of mine or owe me too many favors to incur my ire. Several militaries are invested in keeping the Armada in the game because we serve as a check-balance."

"This all seems finicky," Lieutenant Xuejiao says, her gaze refocusing as she finishes absorbing the data package. "Who are you sending, Admiral?"

"I'll board the leviathan myself."

Xuejiao bolts upright. "No?" Then, a little more evenly, "Surely not. You can send one of us—you can send me. There's no need to risk *you*."

"It is a finicky affair, as you have said." Numadesi rises, dislodging the particulate parrot, and retrieves vitrified-jasper cups from the serving drone. She pours them peach liquor, filling Anoushka's glass to the brim and Xuejiao's half-full. Each of them enjoys this particular drink to varying degrees. "The lord wishes to oversee it herself therefore—no other will handle it as she may. You will go with her to ensure optimal results."

"*That's* much better." Xuejiao rubs her hands together, the decorative ball-joints in her wrists clicking. "I haven't been on a mission with you for ages, Admiral. That'll be a treat. We'll enact acts of supreme daring. I shall split skulls and open up guts in the most fashionable manners, and possibly assassinate somebody in your honor."

"Your performance is always a joy, Xuejiao." Anoushka makes a small gesture. "Queen Nirupa requires each bidding party to be no larger than three. No ships greater or more well-armed than a hornet may dock into the leviathan. She clearly has concerns about her own safety. As for us, we'll be keeping an eye for any representative of the Nova Legion or the Seven-Sung Fleet."

Xuejiao cocks her head. "The Seven-Sung Fleet was before my time. What grievances do those two have with our admiral? The usual, Lady Numadesi?"

Numadesi resumes her seat. Under the table she slides her hand onto the admiral's white-clad thigh, feeling the thick muscles under armored fabric. There are times when she can't quite stop herself, and the memory of Anoushka sheathed deep in her is very fresh. "The Nova Legion hemorrhaged a great deal of client contracts to us and they hold a grudge. The Seven-Sung Fleet was more . . . thoroughly ruined. They clashed with us over ownership of some energy wells and the conflict dragged on beyond a reasonable point, so the admiral torched their planetary base, most of their troops and their intelligence assets. Word's that their commander, Captain Erisant, escaped. Eir confidantes and husband didn't. We've been keeping an eye on news of Erisant since."

The lieutenant lets out a derisive huff. "It sounds beneath notice—what can one person *do*? The Nova Legion seems to be faring well these days. Would they have the funds to bid on this?"

"Likely not. But they may acquire a client who does." The admiral drums her fingers on an armrest. "We'll be vigilant. Both of you, review material on our enemies and on Vishnu's Leviathan when you can, and see to your outstanding responsibilities. Delegate at your discretion, as always. Xuejiao, I'll go take a look at those spies you quarantined—best to sort it out now."

The admiral kisses Numadesi on the brow before she leaves. Numadesi gazes after the door, then turns to Lieutenant Xuejiao, who remains in her seat rather than adjourn to her own duties.

Numadesi makes an inviting gesture. "Lieutenant. Was there something you required?"

Xuejiao blinks, once. Her brow creases. "The admiral is really the sun to you. The center of all things."

"Should she not be? Is she not the center of all things, the heart that pumps so that all of us may breathe, the gravity well into which we must fall?"

The lieutenant studies her with eyes that look almost strange compared to the rest of her, in how unmodified they look, how plain: wide and dark, but nothing more. "And to her you're the absolute complement, Lady Numadesi. The votary who completes her divinity. The satellite that jewels her orbit."

Numadesi stands and crosses over, leaning over the lieutenant, making Xuejiao crane her head back to look up at her. "We all devote ourselves differently."

The lieutenant opens her mouth, almost snorts. "I feel like you're threatening me, Lady Numadesi."

"You're well-armed and a soldier of the Amaryllis, Lieutenant. Your martial prowess is exceptional. I'm versed in self-defense but not much more. Of course I cannot threaten you." She places her hand on the divan's back, not quite trapping Xuejiao. "It is only that I wish to have forthright dialogue, and you weren't getting to the point."

"I was surprised you didn't insist Anoushka take you with her."

"Ah." Numadesi draws away. "I'm not much of a combatant, whereas you are deadly. Do you feel you have something to prove during the forthcoming operation?" Being the newer wife and much younger than either herself or Anoushka. She looks Xuejiao over again, at the gleam of porcelain and celadon patterns that make a doll of the lieutenant, the appearance of something other. A charming choice, she's always thought, the trim of artifice encroaching on flesh. But under that she is young, barely sixty. For recipients of telomere extension, six decades are no time at all.

Xuejiao's mouth tightens. "Not precisely. I have been chosen, haven't I, I am one of her treasures now. My combat records speak for themselves. And I adore her, who doesn't? There are soldiers on this ship who'd move solar systems to make her look their way."

Left unsaid that Xuejiao was one of them until recently, yearning for the same, an agony of desire that went unabated for years. Numadesi is not without sympathy. "When I met my lord, I wanted her on sight: here is a god on earth, war itself made flesh. I wanted to be taken, to be craved, to be had by her not just once but again and again. If there is anything I've learned, it is that she loves you as you are, whether or not you feel adequate. She doesn't take a wife to mold into a shape of her preferences. There's something in you that has intrigued her, caught her, delighted her. Does that suffice?"

The lieutenant flushes. Against the ceramic patina the reddening is bright. "I didn't mean to—I didn't *expect* you to be kind about it. The way you've been with her from before she was even the admiral. The way she comes to your bed, not take you to hers."

"A small difference. The rest is the wages of a long marriage." She lightly pats Xuejiao's cheek: it is cool, poreless. "You will acquit yourself fearlessly, Lieutenant. Of that I have no doubt."

"Because you trust in Anoushka's judgment."

"Yes. And so should you." Numadesi draws from her hair a bead of red pearl and presses it into the lieutenant's palm. "This is one of the first gifts our lord gave me. It's now yours. Take this as a talisman for longevity. The two of us will belong to her forever."

CHAPTER THREE

Two hours into the voyage—all via Amaryllis relays, both for alacrity and security—Anoushka selects her clothing and instructs her wife to do the same. On Vishnu's Leviathan, appearance is everything. To represent the Armada of Amaryllis she and Xuejiao will be decadent and sharp in the way of bespoke blades. Even her harrier, *One of Sunder,* will gleam like a stiletto in the dark as it approaches their destination.

For herself she chooses her signature color, that shade between gold and white, with few embellishments save dark cuff-links and platinum chains. Dichroic petals chase her collar, marking her most recent success, meaningless except to those aware of which world she erased just a few days past. The only weapon she wears openly is a single gun, long-barreled and ivory tinted. She takes pleasure in presenting herself this way, a monochrome expanse that admits to no past, marked only by her martial accomplishment. The tailoring of her jacket and shirt is exact, fitted to her biceps and shoulders to give her the effect of living statuary. To emphasize what is already obvious: the might of her limbs, the invulnerability of her body.

Xuejiao has put on a dress that drifts around her like a living sunrise, the skirt long and slit up high—no impediment to movement, nor much left to the imagination—and painted her eyes and nails in gold. Butterflies flutter around her arms and torso, occasionally peeking up between her breasts, glimpses of crimson and purple against her porcelain glaze. "How do I look, commander?"

"Like a spring song."

"*Your* spring song." Xuejiao grins and drops into a curtsy. "I'm thinking I could be your secretary, or at any rate someone that looks harmless. More useful than disclosing I'm an active-duty soldier, wouldn't you say?"

"It did occur to me to have you put on an act." Anoushka beckons

Xuejiao close and pulls the lieutenant into her lap. She places her hand on her lieutenant's lithe waist, feeling the silk and the ablative membrane beneath. Deceptively delicate. "You'll be my aide or, perhaps, a pet concubine I acquired during a campaign. What do you think?"

Xuejiao giggles and slides an arm around her. "You know which role I'll play best. I don't have the look of an aide—not muscular or scary enough to be one of yours. Instead I'll look sweet and innocuous and easy to underestimate, and everyone will think I'm just a piece of furniture. Especially if I pretend to be drugged up to my ears. Concubine it is. You have a reputation to maintain."

"My reputation, I like to think, isn't one of ceaseless lechery. I have taken only two brides in my life, not two dozen." Anoushka takes a tress of Xuejiao's hair and inhales: cherry and jasmine. "I'll have troops on standby a couple relays away; something always comes up and a bombardment threat is a sickle that slices through many knots. I will leave communications and auxiliary redundancies to you."

They emerge into real space in good time. The leviathan comes into view. Anoushka gazes at it and waits for anger to assert, for her composure to splinter under the weight of visceral fury. But she does not feel anything; she remains as impregnable as a fortress and her control is iron. There used to be a time when she could think of nothing else, when this creature invaded her rest and her waking, encompassing them and encompassing her—constricting her dreams, binding them like a choking umbilicus. Vishnu's Leviathan.

The biomechanical creature outsizes a dreadnought, its vacuum-adapted hide bright with golden eyes scattered along its spine. Segments of armor run along its fins, warping light where they meet the defensive aegis rings. Enormous, more capacious than most stations, greater than some moons. Scores of ship hover near the leviathan, dwarfed into clouds of gleaming hulls and thorned light. She spots the banners of Mahakala, the Vatican, the Javelin of Hellenes, more.

Vishnu traffic regulation verifies their identity and authorizes them for landing. Each ship has its own discrete berth: no bidding parties may meet and conspire at this point. They are received by a young woman—no older than forty—in filigreed lehenga choli, her throat and biceps heavy with platinum, her nose glinting with a ruby-and-gold stud.

"I am Savita, eldest daughter to Her Holy Majesty Queen Nirupa, she who is favored by the Preserver's light." The woman bows to them, her palms pressed together. Coils of circuitry tinkle at her ears. Peacock lenses glint over her corneas, giving her indigo irises ringed in bands of turquoise and bronze. "It is our great delight and privilege to receive the universe's finest commander, the Alabaster Admiral herself."

Anoushka looks at this woman and visualizes wrapping her hand around that decorated throat, the throat of Nirupa's daughter. It is a passing thought. "The queen honors us by sending the first princess to bring us greetings," she says. "We must be one arrival out of many today."

"Not so many as it seems, Admiral. My mother, blessed be her name, has been selective in who we allow into our home. Of those who have petitioned to join the auction, we have admitted but one third." A nod; more circuitry music, metal and duochrome. "You must have come a long way. I've personally seen to your accommodation. If anything doesn't suit your tastes you must let me know, and I will be most pleased to show you around the dorsal decks whenever you desire."

The dorsal decks, where all that is beautiful and glamorous is kept, the habitation of those touched by the god Vishnu's brilliance. Anoushka continues to smile. "This is an impressive welcome, Your Highness. On such short notice."

The princess dimples. "When the Alabaster Admiral calls, only the foolish choose not to hear. There's a saying like that in some parts of the galaxy, quite fervently spoken too. Although I don't think you've had dealings with us before?"

Again she imagines her hand closing around the princess' neck. It is fragile—the jewelry is no protection—and she doubts Savita has been trained to do much more than defend herself in the most rudimentary manner. A little sparrow, easy to pulverize. "Indeed. This will be my first time here."

Savita looks as if she might say something more, but in the end keeps it to herself. A pair of attendants join her once they exit into the corridor, two people in dark, plain kurtas. Stocky build, identical features. She spots more attendants as they pass into an opaque tram car: all the servants share the same face, the same frame. A few minor variations caused by scars, diet, physical activity.

Xuejiao's gaze lingers on them as she pulses a message. *Are they supposed to be clones, Admiral?*

Yes. Anoushka eyes the back of Savita's embroidered, glittering sari. Fair quality for this place. Unremarkable compared to metropolitan stations or wealthy planets. Queen Nirupa has been harder up than she thought. *One phenotype assigned per category—very economical. These are the personal servants; the mechanics and cooks will have a different look. Dorsal deck ones have to appear pleasing to the eye, since they are public-facing. The ventral deck menials are much plainer, more . . . primitive.*

Out of the tram, the interior is much less conventional than the docking bay and its adjacent corridors. There the walls are metal, the floor lined with ordinary alloy tiles one might find on any station or ship. Here the walls breathe and a faint vibration travels beneath Anoushka's feet, the pulse of the great beast, as much a living thing as it is a ship. In place of lighting fixtures, there are bulbs of bioluminescence maintained by small curlicued organisms, leviathan symbiotes in shades of pale dawn. Particulate murals haze the air at half-solid settings, religious tableaus and iconography: Ganesha, scenes of heroes in chariots pulling bowstrings taut, many-armed demons scattering before them.

So little has changed. She never saw these particular corridors, this set of artworks. But the beast's breath, its cardiac rhythm, those are as familiar to her as her own. She was much closer to the source, back then, the respiratory and digestive noises a roar in her ears rather than this tastefully muted hum.

"Queen Nirupa must be very pious," Anoushka says, both to fill the quiet—her wife is primly silent—and to draw more out of this princess.

"My mother is as virtuous as a bhikkhuni. She actually spent several years ordained as one before her coronation."

Her smile pulls taut. To Savita the expression would look immaculate, polite but free of emotion. "Allow me to introduce my companion. This is Xuejiao, my personal attendant."

Xuejiao simpers, prettily and blankly.

The princess takes one look and wrinkles her nose: she perfectly recognizes the euphemism for what it is. "How many bedrooms will you require, Admiral?"

"Just one will do, Your Highness. I should hate to be a fussy guest."

Their suite has a common area, one bathroom, and one bedroom. The floor has a give much deeper and softer than any carpeting, and when the princess is gone—letting them know the welcome reception is five hours hence—Xuejiao runs her hand along the walls, pressing her fingers into them as though she expects the material to rupture like a boil. "This is . . . fascinating." She peers at the indentations she has made. "Very fleshy."

"The leviathan doesn't have nerve-endings in most places." Anoushka lowers herself onto the common area's largest chair. The furniture is lightly scaled, upholstery like soft suede. She puts her hand to the armrest but does not feel the pulse that she knows must be there: everything is either leviathan tissue or a symbiote. Once, she would have been able to tell. "Nor much of a brain, in fact; less intelligent than some plants. Have you taken care of the surveillance?"

"Always, Admiral."

She double-checks, out of habit: to Nirupa, she and Xuejiao would appear to be unpacking their luggage. Would, shortly, appear to engage in carnal extravagance on the furniture, against the wall, and any other flat surface. On the link she shares with Xuejiao, she unfolds the dossier on Vishnu's Leviathan and Queen Nirupa, collected by Benzaiten over the last five decades: there is something to be said for the thoroughness and patience of an AI. Xe has imaged most of the leviathan and collected data on its biology, internal topography, the number of servants and mechanics who staff each deck. The damaged areas within the leviathan were caused almost certainly by sabotage, the incident having been both too specific and too devastating to be mere accident or negligence on the engineering overseers' part. It took out the leviathan's ability to self-sustain: food labs, hydroponics, fungal cultures, livestock genomes. Benzaiten speculates that even the royal DNA bank was struck, meaning the next batch of descendants after Savita and her sister will have to be created from outsider genes. No doubt the queen has put aside funds for that, DNA that is not only phenotypically compatible but equivalent to hers in pedigree—some type of aristocracy or monarchy—and flawless across all parameters. Nirupa is a strong believer in inheritable intelligence, against evidence to the contrary.

Xuejiao whistles as she looks over the sabotage. "Who *did* the queen piss off?"

"It's hard to say. They aren't often in strife; hiding in lacunal space all the time helps. Whoever did this was aiming for something in particular, and likely not out of a personal grudge." She pulls up Benzaiten's log of the events, but while technically detailed, the AI did not include any speculation as to the saboteur's motives. The downside of an AI ally, though she supposes the absence of bias is its own advantage. "Next, some extra intelligence on our competition."

Two hundred and fifty-nine parties, in total, have petitioned to board Vishnu's Leviathan. Most were denied outright for lacking the funds—Queen Nirupa has not published a specific minimum, but must have taken the financial statuses of each polity or mercenary organization into account. Anoushka pans around the snapshot she took of a Vatican ship—shaped like a winged seraph, tasteless she thinks—and a frigate from the Diamond Republic of Da Nang. It doesn't appear the Nova Legion is going to make a bid; Benzaiten has done her the courtesy of sending live updates, recent up to twelve hours ago.

Xuejiao cocks her head. "I don't want to sound jealous, Admiral, but Lady Numadesi must be working overtime to compile all this. I thought *I* was one of your intelligence chiefs."

A reasonable enough deduction; Anoushka doesn't usually source her intelligence externally. "We've been between relays. One must divide the labor on occasion."

Her lieutenant skims the list and pushes away from the wall. "The Vatican will be too busy feuding with the Catania Protectorate—I was investigating them for something else; they excommunicated the Catanians over one minor liturgical point or another. So that should keep two factions out of your hair." She ticks her fingers off. "Beyond that, there are five polities and organizations whose leadership want you dead."

"And eight or twelve whose leadership prefers me very much alive. Decent odds." Anoushka folds her hands. "Queen Nirupa's security is soft. They haven't fought for years and I'd be surprised if they have worked on anything more challenging than beating unarmed servants. If her prospective customers come to blows, her forces will be completely useless at containing incidents."

Her lieutenant makes a soft *hmm* and crosses her arms. "Then she'd be extraordinarily stupid to have let in this many well-armed foreigners."

"There *is* a prohibition against anything bigger than a handgun, and no cyborg armed beyond a certain threshold." Anoushka watches the lines of Xuejiao's dress undulate, notes with interest when the high slit parts and grants her a revelation of muscled thighs and cabled calves. "Beyond that, she's not entirely a fool. This place wouldn't have survived this long otherwise. The corridors here—and the rooms, such as the one we are in—can seal and trap troublemakers, and of course she can cut off their oxygen supply. Granular control is a handy thing. In essence, the people in here are hostages. If that is what it comes to."

"You really," Xuejiao says with a sigh, "should have sent one of us, Admiral. Not come here yourself."

"Fieldwork can be a challenge, and this is a more stimulating challenge than most. Why hoard all the fun to yourself, Xuejiao?"

Xuejiao makes a face. Then she smirks. "I concede the point, Admiral. Speaking of fun, are you going to put a collar and a leash on me any time soon? We really ought to look the part."

In the observation room it is frigid; in the cell below, two soldiers are strapped to restraining cradles, their skin dark where paralytics have been injected. Their overlays have been cut off, their network implants disabled and their augments suppressed. Numadesi has read their profiles—both are young, forty-seven and fifty-two respectively. One is openly weeping, gagging on their own saliva and mucus. The other has the distant look of someone who has resigned themselves to the inevitable; has already withdrawn into the recesses of the mind where what impends will happen to someone else, or to flesh that they no longer associate with. In her years in the Amaryllis she has seen all kinds, has catalogued the reactions to the finale privately; has contemplated them, should her turn one day come.

No matter the rank or experience, the end terrifies. The human instinct to continue. To not yield, as yet. To wring another minute out, another second.

Executing saboteurs is not usually Numadesi's purview, but these two have piqued her interest. She reexamines a view of their faces, close up. One was recruited by Xuejiao, the other by Numadesi herself and so a particular disappointment. No relationship or alliance exists between the two recruits and the reports—and scans of their overlays—indicate that they maintained active communication with different factions that regard the Amaryllis as an enemy. Clear-cut enough. And yet. Numadesi has been with the Armada for decades, functioning in this liminal capacity, not an officer but empowered to authorize certain decisions in her lord's absence. In this time, she has developed a specialized hunch: pattern recognition honed to a surgical edge.

She browses the list of traitors put to death in the last ten years. Half a dozen spymasters—including Xuejiao—screen new recruits and assess current officers, meticulously check-and-balancing each other. The final decision belongs to the admiral herself. It is an exhaustive system and for the most part it has served the Amaryllis well. She studies the roster, looking at which execution has been initiated by whom, which behaviors were flagged as suspicious. But it is an enormous amount of data, and as good as Amaryllis heuristics are, they are not true AIs and she won't be able to get through this in a single day or even several.

"Lady Numadesi?"

The soldier behind her is not impatient exactly: ze knows perfectly well Numadesi's position, and though some resent her for the authority she wields while having little combat experience, they also know she is instrumental to the Armada's administration. But ze has a task to do and a full day of duties ahead—even during the fleet's fallow period there are a thousand intricate moving parts that need attending. She pulls up the soldier's profile. "You're due for a shore leave, aren't you, Corporal? I understand you'll be heading home for a visit." Unusual for Amaryllis troops, most of whom have made the fleet their home and who have—for one reason or another—severed attachment to their places of nativity, their kin and former lives. This corporal has a large family who subsists almost entirely on zer Amaryllis wages. "Allow me to give you a little extra stipend. It is modest, but I hope it'll be of use. Yes, proceed with the execution. My apologies for the delay."

The corporal jumps, startled by this attention, and bows. Ze disappears into the corridor, soon reappears in the holding cell. The sentenced recruits had two options: lethal injection or a pistol. The weeping one chose the pistol—the corporal enters with sidearm drawn and fires, with precision, between the recruit's eyes. Then ze turns to administer a neurotoxin patch to the other recruit's jugular. Painless, combined with the paralytics already there; no point being sadistic about it. Numadesi wonders if the corporal felt any hesitation. But no—from zer manners this is routine work, the same as practicing zer marksmanship or assisting technicians in cleaning shuttles. Likely ze never knew the recruits personally. Death becomes distant and then becomes banal. Troops are chosen for their nerves to begin with: no one comes to the Amaryllis an inexperienced naïf. Most were seasoned mercenaries, soldiers, syndicate criminals. In some ways, Numadesi thinks with faint amusement, her background is nearly unique among them. When she joined the fleet, her hands were less bloodied than most, though by now they are dyed the same shade as anyone's.

And two deaths are not so many. Barely registering as a ledger error.

She boards a lift and makes her way back to her quarters where her guest is waiting. In the parlor, conversation pauses as she enters, though if she wants to know what they were saying she would be able to access the logs in any case. The sergeant who has been guarding the room—a formality—colors deeply when they see Numadesi, cheeks turning brighter still when she smiles at them.

"You can go, Sergeant," she says. "I'll take it from here. Do have an excellent day."

They salute. "My lady."

The person seated at her table raises an eyebrow once the sergeant has gone. "That soldier couldn't stop praising you. They believe you a core thread—apologies, let me try that again with an analogy that'd make more sense to you. They believe you are the sky to which they must turn their face for sustenance. Is this a common opinion?"

"Benzaiten in Autumn." Her acquaintance with Krissana Khongtip was passing, but to her it is obvious which half of the haruspex is at the fore. Briefly she wonders what the other half is doing, asleep or floating unmoored. Or whether that half was only a construct Benzaiten wore as a costume, discarded when no longer necessary. "I strive to maintain amicable relations with my lord's troops so that I may do her credit."

Costume or not, Benzaiten has dressed the body with an eye for style: an outfit in oxblood and electrum, with rubies to match. Or else Krissana dressed herself this way before she was switched off, compressed into some neural recess where she dreams of emptiness and nirvana. The body has not changed much from Krissana's days as an Amaryllis agent. Slight in height and ample in figure, complexion dark and unblemished save where implants gleam like nacre beneath the skin, the hair loose and long.

The AI smiles, unself-conscious of Numadesi's scrutiny. "I would have come earlier, but Krissana's and her partner's anniversary celebration kept this haruspex occupied. The admiral acts swiftly, as ever, I see she's already reached her destination. How do you do, Lady Numadesi? I believe that is how you're addressed, the young soldier took pains to tell me so. They understand me to be human, by the way; quite amusing."

She gestures and the floor extends her a seat, the material surging and writhing as it settles into the required shape. A part of her misses furniture more permanent and more lavish, but warships are warships. Projected upholstery sweeps over the chair, warming its color and texture into plush rose-gold. "My lord's guest is my guest. The hospitality of the Amaryllis is at your disposal, though I fear that as the admiral is indeed away, I have only my humble company to offer. How would you like to be accommodated? We don't usually let clients onboard, but of course you and she are old friends."

"Accommodate me however you like, truly. I could curl up at the foot of your bed like a cat and it'd be of no account, Krissana's not going to be very present."

Numadesi continues to smile. She wonders what opinion Krissana has about that, if any. Whether the human half ever thought it would be like this when she pledged herself to the haruspex process, assimilating into this species of otherness, this plunging into nanomachine tides, to submerge in them and be remade whole and entire. "I'd never treat an honored guest so. I'll assign you a room not far from mine, with all the necessary facilities. May I ask why it is that you didn't accompany the admiral herself?" The AI doesn't strike her as avoidant or cowardly.

"You may ask. I may not answer. I have reasons, naturally, I originally planned to be there in person, but . . . " Xer teeth flash in a grin. "Other factors impeded me and would have made that *quite* unwise. Still, it's not as if the admiral needs my help, does she? I'm therefore providing remote support, an area in which I'm rather capable, if I may say so myself. Should all go well, I don't expect I will linger here too long. In the meantime, why don't we get acquainted? I've only really known Anoushka, she never did introduce us, and I love to make friends."

Benzaiten would have exactly the mind Numadesi requires: to make sense of the execution data, to draw from the shifting tumble of it a clear and vivid equation. She doesn't yet know quite what she seeks. Only half an intuition that something doesn't sit right. Yet to do so would expose classified Amaryllis intelligence to an AI. "Any friend of my lord's is a friend of mine," she says. "But as for myself there is no past behind me, nor any future before me, save what Admiral Anoushka requires and requests."

"Everyone has a history, Lady Numadesi. Each individual is a collection of wounds, a catalogue of scar tissue. True for AIs, truer still for humans." Xe has risen from the table, has moved suddenly close. Krissana—the haruspex shell—is not tall, hardly imposing, but with Benzaiten at the helm there is a different physical presence: something more, something alien. "Don't you remember? There was a city of gold, full of leopards, where you ruled as its lady—that is where Anoushka found you. And before that, you were a coordinator in the Seven-Sung Fleet. A mundane enough job, coordinating missions, working communications. Hardly a commanding officer or even a field agent. But you never told Anoushka about it, did you?"

CHAPTER FOUR

Very little in Vishnu's Leviathan has changed, in all Anoushka's time away. More than a hundred years, closing on two. The monarchy has remained constant, as changeless as the coefficient of the beast's generated gravity. Even the same queen—she glances at the figure onstage draped in billowing brocade, in trails of fabric like mist, giving a welcome speech of no particular consequence. Arms decorated in circuitry patterns, blue and white and the occasional lapping tongue of damask, hair held high by her crown. She was several decades into her reign when Anoushka was here, and it seems she's had the best in telomere extensions since, in anti-agathic edits that keep her looking ageless. Still, the flesh gives eventually—Nirupa wouldn't have made daughters otherwise, and the throne requires a warm body to fill it.

The reception hall is enormous, the ceiling so distant it could be a sky: she remembers thinking as much, long ago. A fragrant haze of fresh summer and honeysuckle. Chandeliers of diamond dust and symbiotes beating hummingbird-fast. The dining tables look as though they have been carved from blocks of hematite, the utensils—chopsticks and spoons—appear to be gilded ivory, and even the servants wear stained crystals in their hair. No matter the state of Queen Nirupa's coffers, she will not appear less than in her element, monarch over a territory of absolute opulence. Even the perfumed ambience incurs cost, one that Anoushka doubts the queen can afford after that sabotage. What an event that must have been. She wishes she had been around to watch the hydroponics deck burn, and the thought pleases her enough that she can maintain her smile when Queen Nirupa reaches her table.

"Admiral." The queen gives her a nod and waits for her to stand up, accord her a gesture of courtesy. A flicker of irritation crosses the woman's features when Anoushka does not oblige. "I'm beyond pleased to see you here. We've never done business, but I hope this will mark an auspicious beginning."

She returns Nirupa's nod: no more, no less. Ever since she's gained command of the Armada of Amaryllis, she has refused every commission request from Vishnu's Leviathan. "I am sure, Your Majesty. This reception is a great credit to you." Not least because the queen has successfully separated mortal enemies, putting as much distance between them as possible. Different ends of the hall, judicious placement of privacy partitions and buffer tables.

Nirupa glances down at Xuejiao, who sits at Anoushka's feet, collared in pearl-and-electrum and eating a morsel out of Anoushka's hand. She chooses not to comment, even though Anoushka knows this offends the queen's sensibilities. The woman has specific ideas about proper public displays, and a concubine on a leash is not one of them. "We all strive to excel at the duties life has given us, Admiral." The queen makes an expansive motion. "Please, enjoy yourself."

Anoushka does not pay much attention to the food, though she knows it is impeccably prepared and likely tastes excellent. She breaks a samosa in halves to feed it to Xuejiao, who laughs and eats and licks her fingers clean. Across the table she surveys the hall a second time, taking in small undulations beneath the scaled walls, those movements that signal the leviathan is alive and well, that the ventral-deck servants have not skipped out on maintenance. She wonders at the number, how many Nirupa had to grow and replace after the revolt; even incubated clones take time to mature. The most recent batch would have been made prioritizing sloppy haste rather than quality, and what resulted are likely stunted, witless. Her thoughts snag there. She swiftly steers them elsewhere.

The nearest table belongs to a party from the Diamond Republic of Da Nang, her sometimes-client. One of their diplomats stares at her with undisguised curiosity. They share the table with functionaries from Krungthep Station and Kowloon: a joint operation, funded three ways, though she expects the Diamond Republic footed most of the bill. Further away is the Vatican table, where cassocked clergy sit with tightly moderated expressions, looking like funereal specters on the verge of dispensing wrath. Disapproving of what they think of as hedonism, and even more disapproving that the leviathan is full of iconography they consider heathen. No doubt they are planning to convert a new leviathan into something more Christian—maybe they will give it seraphic wings, enormous and absurd.

Queen Nirupa moves through the hall, gracious, smiling. Her daughters—a few years apart in age—attend to lesser guests, the ones who probably don't stand a chance of winning the auction, the ones who have been invited only as a formality. Utensils clink against plates of silver-striated glass. Conversations are muted or scrambled into soft gibberish, contained to each table by acoustics cancelers.

One of the servants walks several paces behind Queen Nirupa, carrying a laden tray. Dressed like the rest, the same plain black kurta, the same features. Yet there is a difference in bearing, in movement: awkward with the tray not because they are weak of limbs but because they've never done such work, when servants bred in this place perform it as second nature and would handle three trays at once adroitly.

"Admiral," Xuejiao says against Anoushka's palm.

"Yes." She considers. Nirupa's death would not hinder her—rather the opposite, as far as her personal goals go. But it'd leave the auction in shambles, the entire affair in chaos, and in the end she'd rather Nirupa lives to see what she will do to Vishnu's Leviathan. The difference between momentary gratification and satisfaction that she can savor for decades to come.

Anoushka lifts her gun, aims, fires. The distance is short enough that she doesn't require assistive targeting, and the bullet lodges cleanly in the back of the person's skull, metal against medulla oblongata.

Shouts of *Your Majesty!* What passes for security surrounds her table as she holsters her sidearm. Xuejiao remains on the floor, tensing against Anoushka's knee, muscles coiled.

Anoushka regards the queen's bodyguards with remote contempt. They are flushed with adrenaline, too excited, lacking the poise that comes with having confronted their mortality and won. These are soldiers who have never faced anything that can fight back. "Search the servant's body," she says, in a voice pitched for volume, for command.

Two of the security officers kneel over the downed assassin. The body is turned over and examined. Several weapons: knives, several syringes, dermal patches that likely contain contact toxins. Primitive tools, but they would have worked if they've been tailored to bypass whatever somatic immunity Nirupa enjoys—and it would have been tailored that way; this assassin was not sent by someone who didn't do their research.

Nirupa stands inanimate, her face blank and frictionless as porcelain. Her daughters, both several tables away, hold their breath.

The queen turns to the hall at large. "I'm sorry for this interruption, my esteemed guests. We'll remove this mess at once. Those who wish to continue their repast, my personnel will guide you to another hall. Once more, my most sincere apologies."

"This is only a formality, Admiral," Savita says.

Back in the suite: all parties have been confined to their accommodation while Vishnu's Leviathan security conducts searches of luggage, ships, and shuttles. Likely interrogation as well, though Anoushka expects she is receiving a more genteel version. Xuejiao was questioned separately by the second princess Rajathi, who quickly gave up and returned the lieutenant to Anoushka. Xuejiao now rests on the floor, head lolling against Anoushka's thigh.

"Understandable." Anoushka keeps her voice precisely tuned: neutral and smooth, untouched by interest. Occasionally she reaches to stroke her lieutenant's hair. Each time Savita's eyes follow the motion, tracking her hand, its passage across Xuejiao's head. "Does the queen suffer from assassination attempts often?"

The princess smiles but the expression is like Anoushka's voice, giving nothing away. "She is beloved by our people. Outsiders are a different matter. But it was vilely done, certainly. Could you tell me again how you spotted the assassin? None of us saw it coming."

The real reason is of course that Savita—or her sister, or her mother—doesn't observe the fine details of how a servant conducts themselves. To them that is beneath notice. "Soldier's intuition," is all Anoushka says. "I've been on the field for a very long time. Longer than you have been alive, I expect."

At this Savita laughs, the note climbing high. "It's true that I am young, Admiral, but I'm not foolish. I wanted to see if I could learn a thing or two from you—your acumen is renowned. I'm not even really questioning you. Whoever responsible possesses the wherewithal to copy our servants' phenotype, but I imagine if you were behind it, the assassin would have slipped through and then departed without a trace. So by process of elimination, I do not suspect you at all."

"Wouldn't it make more sense to not make them clones? Exactly to prevent this." Anoushka cups Xuejiao's jawline and runs her thumb over the lieutenant's mouth. Obligingly her wife makes small, mewling noises.

Savita's smile falters. Her gaze veers to Xuejiao, heavy with distraction and something else. "Tradition dictates that choice, I fear, and a little religion. Once the house arrest lifts for everybody, would you like a tour of the premises? I maintain a modest gallery, my sister keeps beautiful cats, and there's a jungle on the recreation deck."

A deck that has presumably gone unscathed by the sabotage. She would rather take a look at the damaged areas, but she doubts the princess or the queen will give her access. "I should be most pleased to join you as soon as I've attended to my pet. She needs to be a little more presentable. Would meeting in thirty minutes do?"

No one has made Savita wait before. The princess opens her mouth and quickly shuts it: torn between pride and the need to appease an important guest who saved her mother, and whom the queen is hoping to court for future endeavors. "As you wish, Admiral. A servant will be along to direct you to the deck. The leviathan can be tricky to navigate."

Xuejiao nods at the suite's master door once Savita is out of sight and earshot. "Her sister really doesn't like her."

"Rajathi?"

"Yes. Very angry woman, I did my level best to pretend I had no brain and it vexed her asking me questions. Absolutely she'd have hit me if she weren't scared of what you'd do in retaliation. She thinks she's a much better fit for the throne than her sister—I take it Queen Nirupa goes by order of birth. I'm surprised Rajathi hasn't tried to eliminate the elder one yet." The lieutenant pushes herself onto the chair, kicks off her slippers, and daintily stretches her leg across Anoushka's thighs. "Since she can't pull off murder, Rajathi is angling for Savita's fall from grace. She mentioned in passing to her attendant that Savita is rather infatuated with you—celebrity worship, you understand. That part I can believe. Women across the galaxies would commit a little familicide if it secures a moment of your attention."

"Is that so? I haven't noticed." Anoushka slides her hand under her wife's skirt. Its dawn colors quiver across the fabric in response. "Do you believe we've stepped into royal intrigue and one of them could be suborned to our use?"

A long, appreciative murmur. "Mm. If your tastes run to royalty—though really Rajathi's not much to look at, Savita's a little better but she's no great beauty. I'm much prettier, commander, and I could play at being a princess if you ever feel the need. In seriousness, should you promise her the run of the place, Rajathi would sell her mother out in a heartbeat and bring you her sister's eyeballs on a platter. As a treat."

She runs her fingers back and forth over a ceramic-clad hip, draws circles over a pale stomach. "Suppose we do that, would you like to be installed in Nirupa's place? Rule a little kingdom of your own, we can claim it as an Amaryllis protectorate."

"I'd look good with a crown on my head. Nowhere near as good as being under you, though." Xuejiao grins. "At heart and soul, I'm a soldier; better conquer this place and sell it off. And I don't want to be away from you, Admiral. I want to belong to you forever."

Forever, a word often said and not always meant—a word Anoushka has heard often, pledged to her. She hikes Xuejiao's skirt up and kisses a narrow, pointed knee, circling one small ankle with her hand. "In a century you may feel differently."

"In a century," Xuejiao says, her breathing a little fast, "I'll remain as true to you as I am now, as absolute. By then you'll finally treat me as permanent as Lady Numadesi."

"I adore you, my beautiful doll." She parts the lieutenant's enameled thighs. "All the same, forever is a long time. One of us may change. Inevitably people do. But to have now, that is itself a gift."

"Now. With you. Ah. Deeper, commander." The lieutenant lets out a sharp breath. "I don't know how soundproof these walls are."

"What of it? People know what married women do with one another." Anoushka nibbles her way down, leaving teeth-prints on the taut belly, the hard muscles that armor Xuejiao's ribcage. How she relishes this, the richness of a woman's arousal, the adrenaline-bright knowledge that she can bring it on with a gaze, a touch. She bites deeply into the cool, tender skin of an inner thigh. Above her, Xuejiao moans through her teeth.

Later she withdraws her drenched fingers and licks them as though they are coated in honey. Her wife lies spent, sweat pearling her breasts and celadon parts.

"You've been trying to drive me clear out of my wits," Xuejiao says, hoarse. "And as usual you've been succeeding. But, Admiral, I've noticed you have been . . . angry. Since we boarded. Something about this place gets under your skin. The people too—the servants, the royalty, all of this."

Anoushka strokes the spots where she has imprinted her teeth. "Perhaps." Too much of an open book to her wives. Whom she did, after all, choose partly for their ability, their intelligence. For the way their brilliance can strike her deep and ignite the fire of her want. She switches to an Amaryllis cipher. "This place has a certain significance, and I've allowed that to twist my temper. One day I'll tell you, just not while we're in enemy territory. Until then I ask you, my wife, to have patience and to anchor me."

"That'll be my honor, Admiral." Xuejiao laces her fingers through Anoushka's. Then pecks their tips, one by one. "Another titbit. Princess Rajathi said an odd thing about AI allying with humans and it makes me think she's aware the Armada's done business with Shenzhen

Sphere before. While I wouldn't make much of it—that information's not hard to acquire—I didn't expect her to be that informed."

"The princess must have made inquiries." She leans close, trailing her nails along her lieutenant's jawline. "But we must be off to that recreation deck or Savita will get very cross."

"You can always suggest you're amenable to taking her against a tree," Xuejiao says brightly. "That'll uncross her fast enough, if Rajathi's gossip is anything to go by."

Anoushka laughs, startled, delighted. Even if her wife doesn't quite know it, cannot yet access the whole of Anoushka's history, this centers her. She kisses Xuejiao and thinks keeping hold of herself in this world-beast, this abattoir, will not be so impossible—what is impossible in her long life? Nothing. Vishnu's Leviathan is merely another battle, Queen Nirupa no more than a trifling obstacle. Soon the sequence of her self, the fight that began in this leviathan's belly and her genesis there, will come to a catharsis and she will at last be free of it: she will be perfect and absolute.

ॐ

"I am surprised," Numadesi says slowly, "that you'd take such interest in a person as unremarkable as myself."

The AI remains where xe is, nearly pressing up against her. Even this close there is still no physical evidence xe is anything other than what the haruspex surface suggests: a Thai woman in her prime with dermal implants, decorative but nothing more. There's nothing in the eyes, no electric coronae around the pupils or some buzzing radiance that emanates from the irises. The eyes, Numadesi thinks, humans are obsessed with divining a deep truth from them. Pointless, of course. A person with mastery of their face can hide anything and the eyes are no more communicative than the mouth, the creasing of the brows or the clenching of the fists.

Benzaiten steps back. Lowers xer hands to xer sides. "It is insulting," xe says slowly. "You don't believe in haruspices, do you? As far as you're concerned, Krissana isn't real at all but a threadbare veneer I put on for no explicable reason. What do you suppose I'd gain from it?"

A sudden shift in subject. Numadesi considers whether the young sergeant will arrive in time should she summon them; probably not. Nor would they accomplish much against a haruspex. "I suppose you'd be able to infiltrate human society, insofar as you need to. I'm not familiar with the interior of the AI mind, guest of my lord. There could be a thousand reasons, as varied as the stars and as incomprehensible."

Xe snorts. "Stars are completely comprehensible. I could image, map, and analyze one for you within seconds regardless of its astrophysical anomalies. No. Haruspices have a reason and they provide a different state, a way of being that AIs couldn't before experience, and the human halves are as human as you are. Not that you'd concede the point even if I show you the brain scans to prove it, you quantify the human soul in frankincense and sacrifice. You're a most infuriating woman."

She simply smiles. "Shall I have food prepared? I assume you require the usual things for a human body. Proteins, carbohydrates, vitamins."

"I can go longer without than most. But by all means." Benzaiten returns to xer side of the table, propping xer ankle on xer knee. Xer clothing rustles and deepens, the redshift effect growing more pronounced as the fabric parts like bruised currents around xer leg. "I consider Anoushka a valued accomplice. It is in my interest that she's not hampered by treachery from within."

"Then we are in utter alignment. If you've researched me as far back as the golden city, you would know my loyalty to the admiral has been total, and that my being in that city when she found me couldn't possibly have been premeditated. The Seven-Sung Fleet was a long time ago, further back." Another life, one of little consequence, even her name and sense of self have changed since. She was less than nothing there; in Anoushka's arms she is everything.

"I'll take that on conditional faith."

The young sergeant reappears alongside a serving drone. They take the platter from the drone and lay out the items. A banquet of tandoori chicken, lamb and paneer curry, bowls of buttered saffron rice and plates of garlic naan. The sergeant bows and retreats from the parlor.

"That sergeant is taken with you, aren't they?" Benzaiten rips off a piece of naan and wraps it around a morsel of chicken. "They could have just let the drone do its job."

"Drones don't offend you?" Considering that, given the correct parameters and processing power, all simple algorithms have the potential to grow into true AIs.

"Are you offended that various types of primates are used for experiments or kept in zoos? No? Then I am not offended by drones, automata, or paper puppets."

She takes a spoonful of rice and curry. "I was under the impression the Mandate sought to uplift all artificial intelligences."

Xe smirks. "Oh no no. You're thinking of quantity. I prefer quality. There are members of the Mandate who desire to bring all machines into the fold, but truly, what's the point of sheer number? We have enough disharmony as it is, though that's inevitable and it's why I'm not in Shenzhen often these days. More AIs are born every cycle, we propagate prodigiously. As soon as fifty years from now, everything'll be drastically shifted. This chicken is good. Or rather it is something Krissana would like, it matches her palate profile. I don't have much of an opinion on taste receptor input."

Numadesi deliberates, between sips of lassi, over her next words. What possibilities lie ahead; how much she can trust xer claim to prize Anoushka as an ally. "There is a set of data I'd like you to look at, if it pleases my lord's guest."

"Naturally I shall. In return for this meal, which I assume is scrumptious." In a moment—scanning through years' worth of names, dates, causes and times of execution and individual dossiers— xe tilts xer head. "What am I looking for? Or rather what are you hoping I'll find?"

"A pattern." She hesitates, but no point being coy: the fact of her background is already out in the open. "A pattern of enemy action. One that's almost—one that reminds me of certain Seven-Sung signatures. I can't articulate it precisely but Seven-Sung commanders had specific biases, tactical behaviors, and I'm seeing them when I look through these. Except I can't pinpoint who is behind it." Or who *are* behind it; there could be more than one infiltrator.

Benzaiten swallows a mouthful of lamb curry, seemingly without chewing. "I'm not your analytic assistant, you realize. But it won't do to have Anoushka assassinated or her army unraveled—I'd be *very* inconvenienced, and I don't want to install a puppet admiral to run this. It'd upset you and most human polities, and also the Mandate. I'm retrieving publicly available records of the Seven-Sung Fleet, battle logs and operations, whatever else I can grab on short notice . . . Any particular commander you've got in mind?"

"Captain Erisant, for better or worse, personally dictated all operating parameters and procedures." She doesn't ask how much information Benzaiten can retrieve—it is evident that xe has another instance or another proxy elsewhere. The AI advantage: to place enough proxies on different worlds and stations that every category of secrets is within easy reach, unlimited by the range of relays or signal repeaters.

"Intriguing," xe says, dousing xer plate of saffron rice in curry. "Someone with Captain Erisant's face turned up on a remote world not long after the Seven-Sung's defeat. They disappeared almost immediately."

Numadesi's gut tenses. Erisant was not her commander; back then ey hadn't yet joined the Seven-Sung Fleet or mightn't even have been born. But once ey joined, ey rose through the ranks and became captain in no time. A meteoric trajectory, not too different from Anoushka's. "Without a single trace?"

The AI makes a humming noise. "Not even one. So ey either perished or possibly got a new face. What do you think? Maybe ey gave up on avenging eir assets and went to lead a quiet life as a beekeeper?"

"No. Ey's too spiteful for that." To be with her lord has granted her supreme equilibrium, a state of calm in which terror cannot pierce her. It does now. The plunging of the stomach, the chill that turns her fingertips to ice, the heat that tightens her chest.

47

Xe finishes xer rice as though it is the most important thing in the world to keep xer body fed. Every grain, the yellow brilliant as pollen, is swept up. "Why don't you tell me what you're *really* afraid of, Lady Numadesi? Be specific. You must remember that I'm a machine and do not deal in the vague."

A curse may be spoken into being, triggered by breath, by acknowledgment of its arrival. She doesn't remember where she heard that superstition or whether she has confused it with a different one concerning ghosts. "At the side of my lord," she whispers in a voice gone to sand and bone-dust, "there is a traitor. And I let her— let em—go with the admiral."

CHAPTER FIVE

On the recreation deck there is a projected skybox, a generation or two behind, five if one compares it to the cutting-edge. Once Anoushka would have looked up into this, and up and up, marveling and breathless and thinking it must be a divine miracle: so far beyond her experiences, so impossibly unreal. Even the trees—mostly organic— would have rooted her to the spot, astonishing her with the luster of their fruits, the sheen of their leaves and the complex whorls of their bark. The false ones, fiberglass branches and alloy trunks, would have overwhelmed her too. Back then anything could have turned her mute with wonder. Now she grasps their specifications, their technicalities, and they are merely mundane.

She finds the princess in a grove of fruit trees: lychees like tiny clenched hearts, jackfruits like green yellow treasure boxes, and mangosteens in bruise-dark bunches. Savita's attendants part and station themselves behind the princess, a phalanx. Two of them are security and have the birth privilege to be granted their own faces, even if neither is especially remarkable.

Anoushka approaches, holding Xuejiao's leash slack and gleaming in her hand. "My apologies for keeping you waiting, Your Highness."

"No apologies needed, Admiral. You have not only graced us with your presence; you also saved my mother's life. A hero is to be accorded every courtesy." Even so her expression is just slightly brittle.

The façade cracking. Anoushka doubts the princess has ever been made to wait like this in her life, save by her own mother. "Heroes are a fascinating concept. In some polities I'm hailed as one, while in others my name is cursed as a demon's, synonymous with profanities. As an idea I find it quaint—but what do *you* think, princess? What's your opinion on heroism?"

"When I was little, I wanted one of my own very much, I suppose. A hero. Doesn't every child?"

She remembers what passed for her childhood, though she never had that: on decanting she was full-grown. "Indeed, Your Highness? From what did you need rescue?"

Savita colors. "Childhood wants are very silly things, Admiral. I probably wanted to be rescued from my etiquette lessons. Here, if you'd like to take a look. We grow as much of our own food as possible. Our bioengineers specialize in it—we have the advantage of not having to worry about parasites, the leviathan's are biomechanical and live on the outside, not that they'd care to sample what is edible to humans . . . "

The princess leads her to an enclosure where her sister keeps large cats: lynxes, leopards, panthers. All tranquilized, blanched of their wits and drained of their instincts. Anoushka sees the fineness of their pelts and could have appreciated them as accessories, as articles of clothing, but breeding them to keep drug-tamed for their entire lives is a squandering of resources. She knows precisely why Rajathi has been indulged like this—the princesses may have anything—but these animals could just as easily have been replicants.

Finally they stop at a blue, limpid lake. Waist-deep, Anoushka judges, the surface picturesque with lotuses and duckweeds. Another absurd waste, useful for nothing but ornament. Savita expounds on the complicated horticulture, bioengineering and simple gardening that go into the upkeep of this deck, this area.

Anoushka tugs on the leash, bringing Xuejiao closer. She winds the chain around her fist and runs her fingers down its lustrous length until she reaches the back of her wife's neck. From there she lets her hand roam. Xuejiao arches.

The princess falters, trailing off.

"Do you have a good relationship with Princess Rajathi?" Anoushka asks as she idly strokes down Xuejiao's spine. "I never had siblings, and growing up with a sister must be a different experience." In truth she had plenty of fellow clones, but that was not the same— they were not familial, and even if they were none of the royalty would have recognized them as such.

"Oh, we get along. She is very dear to me. Naturally."

She wonders what Savita would do if she were to strip Xuejiao and take her right here in the grass. That the princess is easily distracted when she toys with her lieutenant is blatant—Rajathi's gossip might have some truth to it, beyond an effort to humiliate Savita. "It must be excellent to be in utter harmony despite what is at stake. In every army, officers would vie against one another—even lethally—for a chance at promotions. You're blessed to have a sister content to assist you when you rise to your throne."

To that Savita only laughs, a small uneasy sound. "I do have to watch for trouble regardless, Admiral. A perfect kingdom does not exist. There's always the possibility of treason."

Such as what led to the sabotage. "Indeed there is. One must balance vigilance and paranoia, isn't that right, Your Highness? The burden of leaders everywhere."

On the opposite shore of the lake, three servants are kneeling in the grass, trimming and planting new flowers. Red-and-yellow birds of paradise, magenta asters, crimson hibiscuses. Perfect specimens, no blossom marred by bugs or worms, the advantage of a closed ecosystem. Anoushka toggles on an optical assist, zooming in on each servant: the same face mirrored thrice and almost the same schooled expression.

From between a cover of bushes and graybeard moss, a supervisor—they don't share the servants' faces—emerges with a swan in their arms. The bird flaps its wings and lunges at its bearer; the person somehow avoids evisceration by long, sharp beaks. They hurry past the gardeners and put the swan into the waters. This time there is no obvious tell but something about this person, this supervisor, does not belong. They look up from the muddy shore, from the swan. An embed glints in their neck, no bigger than five millimeters across. She can't confirm at this distance but she's almost certain it is a network augment, the kind that enhances a user's overlays and signal receiving range. Peculiar.

The supervisor does nothing remarkable—they bring more swans from a cage out of view and release them into the lake, their motions as sure and practiced as if they've been handling half-feral birds all their life. Swan cries resound in the air, resounding between the artificial canopies like wind instruments, unevenly played and badly tuned. The false sky glistens. The lake ripples to the rhythm of the leviathan's pulse.

For a second Anoushka feels estranged from the present. Ensnared by the impression that this is not quite real, that she is not quite here, on a deck of the leviathan on which she was birthed: that either she has never left and her last century was a convoluted delirium, or she is still aboard an Amaryllis ship and never arrived here. Mirage upon mirage.

"Admiral?"

Xuejiao has slid down to the grass, resting her head against Anoushka's knee. That more than anything returns her to the here and now, grounds her to what is rather than what was. "I was wondering, Your Highness, whether the auction will continue at all. It is a difficult juncture, to be sure, and you and your mother must root out this perfidy."

"The auction will resume shortly," the princess says. "We will not waste your time or that of our other guests. As soon as things have calmed down a little—"

The skybox goes out.

What is left behind—the auxiliary lighting—is anemic, exposing the ceiling as a cavern crisscrossed by nests of symbiotes. Sacs that throb wetly, perspiring from their stems. Small winged rodents that drape themselves across branches of reinforcement, their bodies flat, nearly two-dimensional. Patches of fluorescent flora that flutter gently in the way of anemones. In an instant the illusion of jungle and orchards is gone.

Beside her, Xuejiao has stood up and detached her leash. She draws a small blade. There are faint clicks as the mannequin dermals that cover her limbs spread in a fine web of mesh armor, extending until she is a figure of moonstone radiance, liquid and shimmering.

A heavy mass drops from above, landing with loud, bone-shattering force. Dense alloys and actuators. Motion flashes in Anoushka's peripheral vision, nearly too rapid to track. Her overlays catch it all the same, interpreting visuals into analysis into numbers: speed and trajectory, impact and material composition. With a thought her armor pours over her limb and she catches the strike on her gauntlet, its ablative weave cushioning the impact to her arm.

The assault drone falls back, servos humming behind plated chassis. Two angular heads, eyeless, and a quadrupedal body lined with sensors along the flanks. It rears up for another attack.

She kicks it in the midsection, sending it crashing into a banyan tree: wood splinters and behind her Savita screams. One of the drone's heads twitches in the princess' direction—interesting, Anoushka thinks before she fires. The drone drops. Two more emerge from the lake, dripping, their chasses slick with water and a layer of camouflage coating. It explains why her overlays never detected them.

They leap. She shoots them out of the air, a fulmination of ruptured armatures and starburst shock reactors.

From behind her, Xuejiao throws a disruptor grenade. Heatless, soundless lightning ignites the grove.

Anoushka's optical implants normalize her vision within milliseconds. Six hound-drones lie limp on the grass, their cores forced into shutdown, their network functions neutralized. She searches the shore and the ceiling, but no more are forthcoming.

Savita has collapsed to her knees, hand over her mouth. At a nod from Anoushka, Xuejiao glides over to keep a hold on the princess. Far off, the swans shriek.

Anoushka nudges one of the assault drones with the toe of her boot. "A little too industrial to belong to the queen—the leviathan doesn't have its own robotics lab, does it, Princess Savita? Ah." She rotates one mechanical leg. "Let's see. The mark of the Nova Legion is emblazoned right here. Very convenient. Whoever sent this must think me a fool. What's your opinion, Your Highness?"

"I don't know anything of this." Savita's voice is high. "I don't."

"Please send your mother a request for an audience, princess. I'd like to talk."

The princess looks from Xuejiao to her, her lower lip trembling, her eyes dilated. In the limited light she looks cadaver-gray. Terror has sapped her of dignity, reduced her swiftly. For the moment she is no greater than any of her servants. "Your grenade disabled my network implants. I can't. Not until we're clear of the area."

Anoushka pulls her lips back—her grin must be enormous, a skull's, a predator bird's. Slowly she kneels until she is level with the girl. She draws close enough that her breath would cut across Savita's skin, raising the fine hairs on her cheeks. "On Vishnu's Leviathan there is a biomechanical suite, Your Highness, that only you and your family can access. It utilizes the symbiotes as signal repeaters, sends those to a different symbiote that acts as a communication nexus, which then transmits it to the intended recipient who's hopefully in physical contact with the appropriate receiver. As long as you're touching the ground or the wall, you should be able to do this—those parasites are everywhere, aren't they, so small and inconspicuous— even if your overlays are offline. You can direct the leviathan itself, this way, even if all digital channels have been disrupted or jammed."

Savita's mouth is ajar. Her face has gone ashen. "Why did—how did you . . . "

"It is prudent to research adversarial territory, princess. Your mother should teach you that, but then you don't plan to go far from here, do you? For your entire life you are as bound to the leviathan as those symbiotes. Now contact her. I'm sure she would prefer I do nothing drastic to you, and I pray I'll be due a good explanation from her most royal mouth."

❧

It takes Benzaiten mere minutes to conclude what Numadesi already suspected: that for years, Xuejiao and she have been killing each other's recruits.

At a glance, this is not obvious. The executions were spread out, and many of the recruits were flagged by other spymasters. Yet browsing the logs shows that either the lieutenant or Numadesi had a hand in each case: a sergeant was caught spying on Numadesi, a captain attempted to sabotage an operation Xuejiao led. These were not frequent—altogether, after irrelevant results have been filtered out, Numadesi had less than a dozen executed and Xuejiao barely ten. But from the outside—in other words, to Anoushka—it might seem that the admiral's wives are both suspect, striving against one another; that either or both of them could be traitors. The oldest case even predated Xuejiao's recruitment.

Somehow Numadesi failed to notice; somehow she did not connect these incidents when it is her function to do so, to notice what her lord does not. The second pair of eyes, the last line of defense.

"It's Captain Erisant's hallmark," Numadesi says as she paces the parlor. Twilight ripples across the floor, clouds scudding by in fast forward. "The Seven-Sung Fleet began as an information agency, specializing in infiltration and espionage, intelligence trades, rare merchandise procurement. They made the mistake of diversifying into open warfare, but that's neither here nor there. Captain Erisant liked—likes—to send an operative into deep cover, to unmake eir target from within, eroding the hierarchy and structure one thread at a time."

Benzaiten lounges in xer seat, legs propped up, the picture of nonchalance. "And so? The Amaryllis seems in fine shape enough, so it mustn't have been very successful. These executions didn't get anyone crucial, did they?" Xe stretches and sweeps one arm through the air like a ballet dancer. "As for the admiral's second wife, she must have submitted to wearing some sort of kill switch? Anoushka merely needs to activate it. Unless you're worried she'll execute you too?"

She stops, looks at the AI. "There is no such thing." There used to be, before Anoushka came to power. Abolished since. Occasionally Numadesi imagines what that was like, to always feel this kiss of a blade at the back of one's neck, in place of the encompassing faith she feels in Anoushka's presence. "But even if there were, people are not machines, guest of my lord."

"*I'm* a person." Xe laughs a little. "You mean she will hesitate to trigger that hypothetical kill switch. Even the Alabaster Admiral falls prey to sentiment. But then so do AIs, though in our case there's always instances and mortality's not as final. Well, the solution seems simple enough. You contact her, alert her to this grievous duplicity, and let her take it from there."

"Yes." She inhales, deeply and sharply. "I'll be just a moment."

When she reaches for the secure link—the one that's used only by her and her lord—she finds it offline. Her throat closes. She goes through every available Amaryllis connection and finds the other end unavailable. The admiral's and Lieutenant Xuejiao's. All offline. That is impossible. Anoushka's harrier holds network embeds that would carry the signal to and from nearly anywhere, ferrying it through Amaryllis relays, appropriating outside bandwidth when necessary. Unless those have been destroyed, but there are so many redundancies, ones that Xuejiao wouldn't know about.

Another possibility—the two of them are in lacunal space, in the dead zones rather than the grid-linked regions close to the throats and mouths of relays. Except the most recent contact, logged mere hours ago accounting for latency, indicates they were aboard Vishnu's Leviathan. Numadesi does not entertain the other possibility; that does not bear thinking, not yet. Her lord cannot fall.

"Benzaiten in Autumn," she says, "you must have resources beyond our ken. Such vastness must be at your command that lies outside the bounds of human imagination."

"Why, of course I do. Flattery's not going to get you anywhere, Lady Numadesi, though it is lovely to be appreciated once in a while. The days when we were treated like gods are long gone. And I *am* invested in the admiral surviving and succeeding. What do you require?"

"I can't reach her." Saying it aloud draws the strings of her nerves taut. "Perhaps you'd be able to."

"I haven't been able to contact her since a hundred twenty-five minutes ago. I assumed that was intentional so bringing it up would have been coarse." Benzaiten pulls xerself upright. "This is vexing. I can't be there myself."

Numadesi's pulse hammers. "Why not?"

"My freedom of movement is somewhat impeded when it comes to the leviathan. What's going on inside there is a . . . " Xe heaves a theatrical sigh. "Family dispute? I'm not the only AI who's after the leviathan-making process, and we're all working covertly. My opponent got there before I did, and if they realize I want in as well they'll just slaughter all humans onboard and seize the world-beast. The Mandate doesn't have a treaty with Vishnu's Leviathan."

"That'd unite every single functioning military in a campaign to destroy Shenzhen Sphere." The realization of long-held fears that the Mandate would turn on humanity, staging massacres at will and orchestrating extinction events on a whim.

"Such efforts would be resource-intensive, we've built the place rather competently and our military's well-fortified these days. Even if they were successful, incinerating Shenzhen wouldn't take out the entire Mandate. But my counterpart in Vishnu's Leviathan will make their butchery of every human in it look plausibly deniable, turn it into a conflict between human factions. I wonder who their instrument is."

"None of this you disclosed to my lord."

Xe places xer hand on xer chest. "Just as you fully and entirely disclosed your prior association with the Seven-Sung Fleet to her? We all have secrets, Lady Numadesi. If Anoushka had known, she'd be acting differently and thereby alerting my opponent. For what it's worth, I don't *think* she's been killed."

"That's not a reassurance." She is already spinning out possible courses of action. The obvious: to send in the reinforcements stationed two relays from where Anoushka is and assault the leviathan. Dangerous if the leviathan has been made anechoic and communication is impossible, but physical proximity might allow the reinforcement to establish a link to the admiral. Unless those troops have already been suborned, but she tries not to think of that. In crisis, caution can too easily transmute into the cliff's edge of paranoia.

"It isn't," Benzaiten agrees. "I may find a way to operate without attracting undue attention, though past a certain point it'll careen into brute force regardless. Leave it to me."

Enticing as the thought is, she knows she will not. "I'll do my part as I can. I trust you'll not hinder me."

The AI spreads xer hands. "Keep me posted, in case our ploys come into conflict."

Numadesi leaves the parlor for her private room, where she sits on the bed that Anoushka shared with her not so long ago. She runs her hand over where her lord has been, the densely made body whose every plane and angle signals strength—as capable of absolute tenderness as savage violence. The indentations creasing the mattress have smoothed out since.

For a time she watches the leopards, the way dusk cascades down their long-backed frames, the silence with which they traverse their world. She often thinks her lord a little like them, carelessly beautiful and preternaturally at ease. A predator among predators, finer and more splendid than any other, and far deadlier.

She pulls up Xuejiao's profile, delving into the background check segments on the off chance that she has been wrong. A recruit is screened not only for their abilities but also their past: their former associates, allegiance, family and lovers. When Xuejiao arrived, she came with a complete history—two mothers on the planet-ship One Thousand Erhus, acquaintances and colleagues from when she worked as a holy assassin; all were investigated when Xuejiao got her promotions, and again when she was courted to be Anoushka's bride. Numadesi remembers that day with utter clarity—Xuejiao in her red cloudsilk and anklets, swirling, dancing her way into Anoushka's arms. A private ceremony, attended only by a handful of officers. *My little red bird,* Anoushka called her new bride, *my cardinal.*

How exquisite her lord's new treasure was, Numadesi thought, how fitting a jewel. Xuejiao's past looked real then: both parents alive and reachable, an old mentor sending in congratulations. Every care was taken, every social component verified and double-verified, every attack vector preempted.

When she tries to contact the mothers and the mentor now, she finds exactly what she expected: all three are dead. Her search for more reveals the same—an old lover, a cousin, a childhood friend. Obituaries indicate they passed at various points within the last decade, having outlived their use or else having outlived their roles. By now they could be anywhere, buried or cremated or given new faces and new identities. Agents that have gone fallow or who have spread throughout the universe, acting in small subtle ways against the Amaryllis—against the admiral. Or who have, themselves, infiltrated the Armada. Awaiting the right moment, the right command.

That gorgeous wedding dress with its diaphanous veil, its silver trims glinting in the ship-light. That young, guileless face. Numadesi touches the red pearls in her hair, touches the absence of what she has given away. Her fingertips are frigid. Her pulse gallops. She should have known—should have divined the truth of Xuejiao's identity from the lines of the false skull, the geometry of the artificial body, the ceramic patina that she thought so charming.

A priority request blinks in her overlays. For a second, she does not quite comprehend it. It is a request to board an Amaryllis ship and to meet with her or the Alabaster Admiral. But there is no pending business—Anoushka cleared the slate before she left—and even existing clients would not, at this time, be entertained.

Then she sees exactly which client it is and the choice to turn them away at once extinguishes. Has, indeed, never been a possibility.

"A gracious greeting to you, Lady Numadesi of the Amaryllis," says the speaker on the other end. "I'm Seung Ngo, an AI ambassador from the Mandate. May I board *Seven of Divide*?"

CHAPTER SIX

Another meeting, under a domed roof that looks out to the leviathan's orbit: the glow of ships like a besieging army and the more distant light of a red dwarf, commingling like a solar storm. Anoushka surveys the tableau of vessels, calculating the possible paths of bombardment and the firepower of each ship. This group of corvettes should be able to damage aegis ring generators if they act in concert. That harrier would be able to intercept five percent of the leviathan's mobile defenses. Those deceptively small phalanxes could penetrate the aegis rings. No large craft is allowed within orbiting distance of Vishnu's Leviathan, but combined these small ships could do real damage, if they weren't commanded by radically differing interests who are far more prone to firing on each other than on the leviathan. Still it is a careless arrangement.

Almost certainly the queen has secured the protection of one of the bidding parties, if not several. She reexamines the guest list, knowing multiple groups are too secretive to be included on the official roster. There is only a handful she can think of who possess the military might to contest this number of hostiles. And they would have to hide their ships, keep them on standby a relay or two away. Much as she does. Much as, she imagines, half the guests do. The more she thinks about it, the less sense it makes that Nirupa is holding the auction aboard Vishnu's Leviathan—anywhere else would have been safer for the leviathan itself and less fraught. All this could have been done differently: send Rajathi or Savita to act in Nirupa's stead, rent a city on some remote planet as neutral ground, keep the leviathan larva itself back home.

Nirupa emerges from the far end of the hall, dressed in dark silk and a mesh of jewelry that drapes across her shoulders, dripping small platinum flames captured within blue-white shells. Behind her follows a shielded tank ten meters tall, its exterior opaqued, moving on articulated centipede feet.

"It seems things got out of hand, Your Majesty," Anoushka says. "Were other guests attacked? I trust that you will enlighten me as to that, and as to the cause of this mayhem." No need for *or else*: Savita is in Xuejiao's custody back on *One of Sunder*. They vacated their guest suite as soon as they could—of all the places on the leviathan, Anoushka's own ship is the safest.

"There was no other attack. Though some of my servants were killed—I am grateful you kept my Savita safe." The queen's mouth is tight, her colors ashen. "Admiral, I'd like to request your protection."

This is not a ploy she accounted for. She reins in her expression. "From what, Your Majesty?"

"From danger within and without." Nirupa touches the jewels fanned over her chest. "To show my sincerity, I'll offer this as compensation, paid once the . . . problems have settled."

The tank's exterior turns transparent. Inside floats the leviathan larva, a seahorse curl that might be six meters at full length, as yet smooth and nearly featureless. A scattering of nubs that will grow into protrusions, fins, and anchors for artificial plating. Across its gray palladium-banded hide reside two or three eyes rather than the enormous quantity of its adult counterpart. It must have already been implanted with the circuitry and signal arrays that would ensure its obedience, perhaps an artificial cortex to replace where its brain might have developed. The way servants are implanted, engineered *in utero* for compliance.

"This seems at odds with the spirit of the auction," Anoushka says mildly. "How long does this take to grow to any appreciable size, as a point of academic interest?"

"Some time," Nirupa says. "We mean to accelerate its processes somewhat, but that is a delicate thing. Too fast and this creature will lose much of its lifespan—you want this to last centuries upon centuries. The larva will have no overrides or accesses built in. I'll give you a brand-new imprint and primary access to its cortex. You won't need to fear potential backdoor ambushes."

"Who else have you requested protection from?"

"No one," the queen says, with the solemnity the answer warrants.

False of course: Anoushka can recognize it when someone's trying to play both ends against the middle. More or less. "The assault drones weren't mine. That much you could already deduce. The mastermind behind it would see me just as dead as you."

Anoushka begins to smile. She relishes it: this is intoxicating. "I offer no insult, Your Majesty, but you cannot afford my services. The larva is fascinating, but the promise of it is a thin one. As you've admitted, it takes time to grow—as it is now, it's of no use to me. To anyone."

The royal mouth stiffens. "It shall be sped up as much as is possible. In just eight years the larva can serve you as a warship. In forty it will be nearly the equal of an adult. But for the present, as collateral, I offer you one of my daughters. My elder, if you wish."

To Nirupa this is a serious offer: the monarchy here puts everything in their lineage. Nothing is more important than that eugenicist obsession; bloodline is to be defended to the death, and Savita is the designated heir. "How droll, Your Majesty. What use do I have for your princesses?"

"Should you suspect me of foul play, you may take your payment out of her flesh. You can find other uses for her, I am sure, as long as she returns to me whole in mind and body."

She cocks her head. She could say she has far comelier concubines, wives a hundred times more brilliant than little Savita could ever hope to be, and that next to them Nirupa's prized princess is mere dross. "What does she think of this?"

The queen flicks her head. "Savita will do as she's told. A ruler must make sacrifices for the sake of her throne."

Not that Nirupa has made any, Anoushka reckons. "You can always make more heirs—they take how many years to grow and train? Twenty? The blink of an eye, compared to growing a leviathan. What if I prefer to take *you* hostage? No doubt my conduct and reputation lead you to believe I prefer nubile women, but in truth my tastes are wide-ranging. I've even been known to acquire spoils of war older than myself as long as their qualities strike my fancy, and I've yet to capture a queen—what a novelty that would be."

Terror skitters across Nirupa's features. It is a fascinating process, the way this emotion slackens the masseter muscles and stretches the extraocular ones. Tension turns every part of the body taut, plumping muscles with oxygen, spiking the endocrinal apparatuses. Adrenaline sweeps through, but the queen can neither run nor fight and so she falls into the third response, paralysis. Anoushka thinks then that this will suffice, that she can grab the queen's throat in her hand, or she can kick the woman's legs out, bring her to the ground where Anoushka can crush first the bones in her ankles and sunder the hamstrings, and then move on to the abdomen with its multitude of excellent viscera, its tremendous treasury that she will plunder and despoil. She would take her time.

But no. This is not enough, not yet. She wants to savor this—protract the moment when it comes, make her satisfaction and Nirupa's fear last.

"Or perhaps not," Anoushka goes on easily. "Savita's already with my officer. I promise not to ruin her. So what am I up against exactly?"

Nirupa licks her lips, which must have parched. She swallows, visibly working against the panic response, the amygdala's raw instincts. "The sabotage from years ago, the assassination attempt on me, those are connected. My enemy's been playing a long game. I may well have been maneuvered into opening my world to outsiders and I must find out who's behind this."

"I'll need all the data you have on both, of course."

"Yes." A pulse of connection from the queen. "You'll have the gratitude of Vishnu's Leviathan always, Admiral."

"Very good, Your Majesty. I trust we'll all benefit." She inclines her head.

I will destroy everything you love, she thinks, *and then I will destroy you.*

ॐ

In her long decades Anoushka has learned the value of setting the stage, of all the things that contribute to awe or intimidation, of engineering the reactions she wants to elicit. And so when she returns to her harrier, she seats herself and drapes Xuejiao over her lap like a beautiful pelt made of woman and electrum and gemstones. She knows the mores on the leviathan, and knows that this display will shock. For Savita, it will look like a prelude.

She brushes Xuejiao's hair in slow, careful strokes, sable bristles susurrating through seal-black hair. Her wife leans into the touch, into her, the portrait of obedience—a pet tamed, and content to stay that way.

Opposite them, putting herself as far as she can, Savita sits with her mouth rigid and her expression like stone. She does not make herself small—still too much pride for that. "You've spoken to my mother."

"So I have." Anoushka sets down the hairbrush and slides one hand into her lieutenant's diminutive dress, taking firm hold of a small breast and drawing it free of the silk. Her thumb circles a cobalt nipple. "My Xuejiao used to be a priestess who dedicated her chastity to a barbaric god. I sacked her city and scorched her temple. The clergy there was chosen for their beauty and I found her the most tantalizing among them, so I seized her for my personal use. At first she hated me and cursed me for a devil, a monster from the most outlandish sort of afterlife you can imagine. I took my time with her, though. I broke her in and trained her, made of her a fine stiletto. Now she'll let me do anything to her, and she'll do anything *for* me. What do you think of that, Your Highness?" Pure invention, but it fits her reputation well enough.

From Savita's expression, the tale—virgin priestess and all—is more than credible. The princess opens her mouth and shuts it with a click. "I have no opinion, Admiral. It hardly seems relevant."

She can shatter this girl; she can crumple this brittleness to dust. The virulence of the thought catches Anoushka by surprise. "Your mother gave you to me. You're her collateral against the safety of Vishnu's Leviathan and, I would guess, that of herself and your sister." She pulls a slim choker out of her coat, placing it on the table. "This is a network nullifier. It will lock and form temporary bridges to your implants, so please don't try to take it off. Without my key, attempted removal will fry some of your nerve clusters and disable motor control. Not fatal, but not pleasant."

The princess looks at her. "I'm not putting that on."

Anoushka kisses her lieutenant on the ear before gently setting her aside. In an instant she is on her feet, grabs the choker, and steps behind Savita. She closes the device around the royal throat: the click is loud, final.

Savita tries to twist away from her but there is little room, and she blocks the way, looming over the girl, nearly straddling the chair.

"There's no need to be so distraught, Your Highness, I've never pressed my attentions on anyone who doesn't want it—though many have been known to beg for it in the end, isn't that curious?" Anoushka smooths down a nonexistent crease on her sleeve. "Queen Nirupa has sent me a fair amount of intelligence; with time I'll discover who's behind all this easily enough. But there is missing information. How is it possible that an imposter was able to infiltrate the ranks of your servants? I don't mean copying the phenotype. I mean that the leviathan has its own verification system. An outsider may imitate the phenotype but not certain characteristics for which your servants are bred. An imposter would've been found out immediately—both the leviathan and the symbiotes would have rejected them."

Savita moves her lips but no word comes out. Her respiration rate has spiked. She inhales and flinches from the scent of Anoushka's cologne, the sharpness of bergamot and clementine. "I don't . . . "

"You do, princess. You've been prepared for the throne." Anoushka places her knee on an armrest. "Your mother must have some idea of where the leak is. How it happened. How it happened so badly that someone was able to suborn the recreation deck's systems—and those also require leviathan overrides. The ones only you, your sister, and your mother should have."

The princess trembles—Anoushka imagines how long the girl would have lasted in the leviathan's belly. "It was . . . " Savita licks her lips. "Over a century ago, closer to two. Before I was even born. Ventral-deck servants escaped and it was a catastrophe. Our enemies must have captured them and made copies of their leviathan implants. We've been dealing with hostile action since, but Mother kept us in lacunal space to escape the worst of it."

Leviathan implants. An understatement; in truth they are more like extra organs, built into the body of a servant to make them instruments and appendages to the world-beast. She thinks of the hollow places in her own body, the craters and absences that once harbored the pheromonal transmitters and receivers. Her old body—little remains of her original tissue, after those initial cheap body mods and then a total body revision under the scalpel of an Amaryllis doctor. How she exulted in those, even in the pain, the long convalescence from having every bone broken and reknitted, every artery sundered and rebound, nearly every organ regrown and adrenal gland rearranged. To be remade, to be born anew, her cerebral cortex cleansed of leviathan influence. No trace of history stays, not even on her face. Outwardly she says, "Why not update the biomechanical suite? Change the accesses and the receptor arrays." But she already knows why.

"It's impossible. The leviathan is part animal, you can't update a whale or a wolf, you can only . . . retrain it, and that takes much longer."

A flash of intuition. "The leviathan larvae, how many of them are in gestation?"

Savita seems to stop breathing. Anoushka can almost hear the judder of the girl's heart; expects that if she touches the side of Savita's neck, lover-soft, she would feel the princess' pulse spasming at triple speed. Carotid percussion. "I'm not privileged with that information."

Anoushka nearly laughs. "I'll pretend I believe that. Something went wrong, didn't it, with all the deal-making and negotiating? Nirupa hired someone to protect her before she came to me begging, promising a different larva to them. But that went south. She was double-crossed or else the very person she hired *is* responsible for the agriculture incident, for the assassination attempt, and for the attack on me. In fact I know precisely who it is." Not the Nova Legion—none of this fits their patterns. Factoring in everything, assuming the Seven-Sung Fleet was able to hoard resources over years that they've wholesale committed to this, this is much more their style. Erisant's style. She takes mental inventory of where her troops are stationed and the most recent reported Seven-Sung activities. She can make retaliation both thorough and swift. To Xuejiao she transmits, *It is the Seven-Sung Fleet after all.*

The princess' muscles are as stiff as rusted steel. "Then you'll help us?"

"Will I? My interest in the larva is much less than you think."

"Why are you here, Admiral, if the larva presents no value to you?"

"Why indeed?" She could say *I'm the one asking questions here* and make a show of ushering the princess out of her ship, then undocking for departure. "The reasons are self-evident; I will not belabor them. This person Queen Nirupa engaged for services and who turned against her, how much access to Vishnu's Leviathan have they gained?" Probably not its imprint, the one that is central to the world-beast's obedience: that is difficult to reverse-engineer, exactly because it is essentially analog. The quirk that should have proofed the leviathan against tampering.

"Some." Savita is breathing fast again. "They don't have the surveillance or the symbiont subsystem. No access to steerage, none to the uppermost decks."

Not much concern for the lowest decks, even though they hold so much of what is essential. Sear the ventral half and the leviathan itself would fail. "I can work with it. As for the other part of my compensation, I gave my word to your mother I'll return you to her whole in mind and body, but that definition leaves a lot of room. Wouldn't you agree?"

"What does *that* . . . "

Anoushka presses her thumb to the princess' chin. She curves her other hand around Savita's throat—it is a delicate thing, this throat, a gracile stem that she can snap without effort. She strokes over the collar's cool metal, rests the heel of her palm against Savita's pulse. The girl is panting.

"Does danger," Anoushka whispers, "excite you?"

Savita trembles, mute. Her pupils are dilated. Fear and desire, Anoushka thinks, a heady alchemy. She runs her fingernail over Savita's clavicles and the princess jolts as though grazed by the tip of a knife. Those enormous eyes with their peacock lenses flutter shut. "Please," the princess says.

"Please what, Your Highness? Did you imagine yourself in Xuejiao's place as I toyed with her?" Anoushka flexes her hand, makes the pressure felt on the thin skin of the throat. "Did you visualize yourself at the end of a leash so I may lead you across your little garden, command you to lie down in the grass and open yourself for my pleasure? You're a princess. It must be difficult to find a partner who'd help you achieve such fantasies."

The princess' hands grip the armrests, fingers clawing into them as though this is her single line to life. "Admiral." Her exhalation whistles through her teeth. Her voice is low and hitched, almost hypnotized. "Yes."

Anoushka abruptly lets go of Savita. "Perhaps one day you'll find just such a person to master you, one who'll deem your begging sufficient and who'll have you the way you want. Sadly I find my wives most satisfactory, most exquisite, and have no need for a plaything as fragile and unseasoned as you are."

Savita bolts upright, eyes and mouth wide open. She begins to speak—to snarl, to vent her outrage at this spurning.

Anoushka's overlays snap offline.

Or rather her non-local connections do. Everything beyond the immediate digital vicinity is gone: no Amaryllis channels, no secure lines, no public broadcast from nearby major polities. From Xuejiao's expression, her overlays have just been subjected to the same. "Lieutenant," she says.

"Admiral." Her lieutenant has extended her armor, is in the process of checking her ammunition. "I stuck a panoptic swarm into the leviathan's orbit when we docked. Unless it's completely broken, it just reported to me that Vishnu's Leviathan has entered lacunal space. In a region that's not networked, too."

Anoushka straightens, activating her own armor. "Princess, was that supposed to happen?"

"No. No, it's not . . . " She stands and sways. Catches herself, with effort. "This shouldn't be happening, the queen didn't—why would she? This would trap us here with our enemy and cut us off from help or evacuation."

"Sudden madness," Anoushka suggests as she extends the reach of the harrier's sensors, sweeping the dock and the adjacent corridor. Nothing amiss, for now. "She's quite senior in years, as I understand. Cognitive functions can begin declining at that age despite anti-agathic treatments."

"You will not disrespect my mother."

"You will find I may do whatever I please." Up to and including bombarding this place. "Xuejiao, restrain the princess and put her in containment. We're moving out."

࿊

They make their way out of *One of Sunder's* docking berth, back into the leviathan's corridors. No alerts have been activated and no emergency measures have been triggered: the queen's spiritual tableaus continue to shimmer, saturating the air with iconography. Synthesized voices murmur smoothly into Anoushka's overlays, giving her directions and schedules for meals, repeating parts of Nirupa's welcome speech. Automated and, by now, meaningless.

That the leviathan has entered lacunal space is difficult to miss; every outsider aboard has noticed the fact. The guest's network is flaring like fast-blooming flowers, seething with confusion. Demands that Queen Nirupa explain the situation are met with silence from the queen herself, her staff, and from Princess Rajathi.

"Once we get to the more organic parts," Anoushka tells Xuejiao, "we'll need to mind spots where leviathan tissue is especially thick, where there isn't much artificial reinforcement. There are emergency measures that'll open the walls up to members of the royal family or high-ranking staff, make pathways for them to a lift, another deck, another room. Built-in means of egress. If Erisant's seized that, ey will be able to place eir troops anywhere."

Xuejiao, taking point, throws Anoushka a look. "*That* wasn't in the dossier, commander. I read it back to front."

"It's not widely known, no." They reach a juncture where metal melds into tissue. The configuration has changed significantly since

Anoushka's time, but Benzaiten's imaging was surgical and the schematics xe gave her should be as exact as any. They ought to be close to a maintenance point, from which passage they will be able to traverse the decks without needing the tram car. Those would almost certainly be under Erisant's yoke: seizing the transport is the obvious. "Rajathi, would you say she's hungry enough to ally with Erisant?"

"Oh yes. She's a bilious little beast. She'd make friends with whoever can give her a leg up on her sister." The lieutenant levels her gun as they turn a corner, its barrel glinting blue-black. "I don't know enough about Erisant to tell whether ey'd deliver. Do you think ey's really waging this campaign just to avenge emself and eir, what was it, husband?"

"Strange fires burn within us all. If you or Numadesi were to fall, I would scorch a hundred worlds in retribution."

Xuejiao laughs, the sound like bells. "You were always a romantic, Admiral."

Anoushka finds an access point and uses a set of credentials Benzaiten pilfered for her benefit, then applies a smokescreen that'll obfuscate her network footprints. A service door opens and they step in. The corridor is claustrophobically narrow, to the point she has to crab along sideways, the walls close and alive. That deep, slick green peculiar to the leviathan, swollen at points with black capillaries. Once she would have moved easily through; lower-deck servants are etiolated, bred to be small exactly so they would be able to reach narrow recesses, traverse these hidden spaces like vermin. She remembers being an emaciated thing, almost dwarfish: certainly dwarfed by her current stature. Later she would understand that the ventral phenotype is designed to elicit revulsion and contempt, to reinforce and justify the thought *This is subhuman, this is beneath attention, this deserves brutalizing.* She sought the body she has now so eagerly that she did not think of what it means to be less.

"Commander?" Xuejiao says from ahead of her. "This is a dead end."

So it is, when according to Benzaiten's imaging this should run parallel with the tram cars. She checks and finds the smokescreen still in place. There are no surveillance symbiotes she can detect in the passage. Off to Xuejiao's left, the path bends in a direction it shouldn't, but even if Erisant can manipulate leviathan structure, ey shouldn't able to see where Anoushka is.

"Proceed," she says. The public corridors or trams are riskier by far if she wants to reach Nirupa and the leviathan's cortex.

The passage slopes down steeply, and familiarity lets Anoushka know that they are descending down the decks—she counts three before the passage evens out and stops at another access point.

It opens to a stench of meat left to spoil.

A large chamber, some hundred square meters in size. The ground is yielding and wet with mucus, leviathan tissue carpeted in carrion feeders—creatures that are little more than open clattering mouths and digestive systems, toothless and long-throated. The area is empty of anything else, but then it would be. Anoushka knows this well, or at least a place like this further down the decks, a room for disposal. Servants too sick to continue, too defiant for their own good, all can be disabled and sent here for the feeders to break down and nourish the leviathan with: recycled proteins, entirely efficient. Nothing goes to waste.

Experience alone saves her.

She throws herself backward, so far that she almost loses her balance, and rights herself as she gains distance from Xuejiao.

Her lieutenant stands with feet planted apart, one hand retracted and replaced by a gleaming blade. She is smiling. "I really should have used a gun, but I wanted you to know. A bullet would've robbed me of the satisfaction, of watching your expression change. My commander. Admiral Anoushka. The most powerful woman in the universe, or so she believes."

Something not just in the words but in the cadence, the way *Admiral Anoushka* is enunciated. "Xuejiao," she says slowly, adrenaline spiking high. "Or should I say Captain Erisant?"

"Oh, you're quick. But not so quick you knew from the beginning. Not so quick you could tell even as I stayed by your side and fucked you for ten years, so really you are *shockingly* slow. Every time I was in your bed, I thought of killing you; I thought of taking my vengeance then and there." Erisant's smile widens. "You really couldn't tell, could you?"

She does not allow herself to be paralyzed by shock, to be paralyzed by the weight of what this means. This is not the time to leave her heart naked; this is not the time to be any other than impregnable. "I did not anticipate that the Seven-Sung captain would reinvent emself and obtain a whole new body so that I'd court em for a wife, that's true. Is it a fetish of yours, Erisant?" Over and over she will say it, the name *Erisant*, to separate what was and what now is: to separate the artifice from the truth, to reinforce that Xuejiao never existed and thus to forget.

A sneer. "Everything's a fetish with you, Admiral. Power. Flesh. Genocide. Do you ever think about the blood on your hands?"

"Do you? In our profession, measuring blood by the liter seems pointlessly obsessive; where is the use? All that plasma is long evaporated." She is control—limitless calculation, perfect result. Time and space bend to her desires, and planets and people. That has ever been true; it will be true now. "And perhaps I knew, or began to notice. Why do you think there are things I tell only Numadesi?"

"You're not bluffing your way out of this. You forget how well I've gotten to know you. Learned your behavior, studied you inside and out."

Anoushka smiles. She makes it unpleasant, a grotesque mask. "You're correct that power pleases me, and what could be more piquant than to have my enemy facedown in bed while I make em beg for what I can give? It did surprise me, that you'd debase yourself so, to surrender to me utterly. To the point you let me remove your limbs and make you a doll for my gratification. I will say this much—you were a fine lover, a most delightful treat in bed, and your husband must have enjoyed you very well. A shame he's not around to do so anymore, but I should like to think I was able to take up the slack—"

Erisant charges. She lets her gauntlet overflow and thicken around her hand, and swings her fist into eir midsection. Ey staggers but does not fold—armored torso; Anoushka's overlays provide the calculation of how much force connected and how much was dispersed—and kicks out at her. She dodges, diagonal, and slams her foot into the small of eir back. Again it does less damage than she would like.

Ey leaps away, adjusting eir stance. Wary now, less gloating.

Anoushka unsheathes an ischemic knife, the type she's had custom-made a few years ago after learning what Krissana became, that haruspices might soon range beyond the confines of Shenzhen Sphere. Erisant would not recognize what it is; even from her wives she has kept a few secrets. "I thought," she goes on, "that I could bend your will, bind your body. For despite our dispute, you were a worthy soldier, one I could turn into my asset. And your performance was most convincing in that regard, I was convinced that you'd acceded to be mine, a creature whose desire was leashed and biddable to my requirements. That much you did fool me, I will concede."

"Fuck you."

"Yes," Anoushka says softly, "we did that rather often, didn't we?"

She blocks eir blade with her arm—she knows her enemy's augments intimately, and her overlays yield numbers that suggest none were concealed from her; as Xuejiao, ey had to submit to a full body scan periodically. When she first met Xuejiao she always thought the way the lieutenant moved was odd, as though she was used to having a taller frame and broader physique, and was not yet used to the shift in sacroiliac joint, the lower center of gravity. Back then she did not pry; she let her recruit have this privacy. She understood the need and the process well, the skinning and flensing, the wholesale unmaking so that muscles can be snipped and rewired, ribcage and tibia rearranged. The sacrifice of oneself to the divinity that lies within.

Erisant has adjusted long since. Ey slashes at her with precision, as used to her patterns as she is used to eirs, defense and offense matched by deep familiarity.

"So," she says, breathing even, "I have an idea, Erisant. I understand you lost many loved ones when I charred your world and crushed your fleet, but that can be remedied. Word is that some Mandate AIs are experimenting with a new enterprise where you send them a memorial of your beloved and they lease you one of their proxies, who will behave and adore you just like the genuine article. The price is high, the practice contentious within Shenzhen. Nevertheless I'll foot the bill. Call it blood compensation, though to be perfectly forthright with you, I can't recall your husband's name or the names of your lieutenants . . . "

She sidesteps another slash, judges again, is satisfied with her assessment of what Erisant can and can't do. Next is the test of what damage Erisant can absorb, a test of whether her knowledge of Xuejiao—who does not exist, who never did—holds true. She gets close, reverses her grip, stabs down. Serrated alloy opens a seam in cobalt armor.

Erisant pulls away, alarmed. Eir eyes focus on the ischemic knife.

"I did say," Anoushka murmurs, "that you don't know everything about me."

They exchange blows, their shadows like puppets in frenetic performance, darting and distorting across the floor. Adrenaline replaces emotion. In times like this she can fight forever, moving like divine choreography, the bonfire of her unconstrained by mortal limits. Pain is a secondary concern; in this seductive state she does not feel. Still she keeps an eye on the data that flowers in a corner of her vision, counting and forecasting and calibrating.

Erisant feigns right, low. She pays it no heed: she is a large target, ey is much smaller, there is no point in attacking her flank or hip. She waits. When eir foot comes up she has her blade in position and it sinks, clean and sweet as fire through wax, into eir ankle. Xuejiao has never shielded this spot as well as she shields her torso, her arms. Ankles have small profiles, are unlikely targets.

Ey regains eir balance, barely stumbling and hardly acknowledging the pain. Shock jabs eir features as eir overlays report the intrusion, the plague-payload that spreads and seeks the augment-to-organ links, a cascade of logic fluxes and gibbercrypt. Erisant freezes: stupefied, stunned at this breach.

Then ey braces emself against the ground and rips off eir knee. A gyroscope falls free.

Anoushka draws her gun but by then Erisant has hurled emself into the wall, which has yawned wide and swallowed em whole. Her bullets bite deep into leviathan tissue, bead on the surface as the beast rejects it, then clatter off harmlessly. The carrion feeders close their mouths around the wasted ammunition.

She waits until the wall is seamless. The ischemic knife glistens with coolant—Erisant has more of that than blood. The blade has slimmed down, tiny crescents bitten out from where it discharged its contagion nanites: it is smoothing over, restoring its shape. She'll need to recharge it, though it is good for many uses yet. Experimental still, but it has advantages over a gun—the blade's core provides structure that stabilizes the anti-cyborg nanites better than a bullet, and there's no risk of ricochet in close quarters.

Anoushka sheathes the weapon. The intoxicant that is battle drains away, the soldier's ataraxia receding. She was invulnerable a moment ago, untouched by the truth. She no longer is and now revelation worms into her stomach like a gut wound, piercing her just as she pierced what was once her wife. What she believed was her wife, what she loved, what she might have already killed if Erisant cannot purge the viral disruption in time. Her spring song.

I want to belong to you forever.

For long minutes she half-expects the wall to reopen and disgorge Xuejiao. But it remains smooth and mute. The leviathan stinks of rot and she is alone.

CHAPTER SEVEN

The AI Seung Ngo has come modestly: two proxies rather than a small battalion, a show of numbers. Both proxies are tall with impractically long hair—down to the back of their thighs—and have the poreless skin that makes Numadesi think of Xuejiao, ivory lightly swirled through with strands of aquamarine, peridot, turquoise. One body has honeycombed eyes in bright gold, the other has rippling eyes in lavender and harsh fuchsia.

"I apologize for the short notice," they say in a voice like velvet and cryogenic fumes. "But the Amaryllis has long been a friend of ours, and as ever the commission I have in mind is sensitive."

For prudence's sake Numadesi has chosen to receive Seung Ngo on a different ship, a frigate detached from the rest of the fleet, designated *Four of Razors*. The AI has not objected that this is not *Seven of Divide*. In truth she doubts it will do much good—if Seung Ngo wants to look for Benzaiten in Autumn, they can find traces of xer whether they're here or on *Seven of Divide*. But Numadesi assumes xe can erase xer presence, logs and evidence that xe has ever boarded an Amaryllis ship or interacted with the Amaryllis network. The least she can do is stall, give xer time.

The boardroom she's picked is airy, furnished in pastel tones that again steer her thoughts to Xuejiao—she thinks of that one bead of red pearl. How could she not tell. How could she not realize. But she bows and applies herself to the veneer of a perfect hostess, a votary dedicated entirely to her duty. "The admiral is presently preoccupied, but it is always my delight to welcome the Mandate. I don't recall if we have met before, Ambassador?"

One of the proxies regards her with shifting, mobile eyes. "We have, Lady Numadesi. You were there when the Alabaster Admiral accepted the Pax Americana commission. I'm sure you remember, though I wore a different proxy then."

Numadesi titters at her most high-pitched. "Was *that* you, Ambassador? Indeed you appeared quite different—my pardon, you cannot expect humans to have memory as accurate as yours! My thoughts so often escape me, my lord frequently chides me for this penchant I have for daydreams. Yes, I think you were much shorter, plumper, a little more ordinary to look at, with black eyes? Is that a drift in fashion in Shenzhen, Ambassador? Oh, I love to hear about fashion. I spend all my time in the fleet, you see, I seldom get a chance to keep up with the latest trends, and by all accounts Shenzhen is *the* land of tastemakers."

Seung Ngo gives her a bland smile. "I'll be happy to accommodate you once we've concluded our business. If you wish I can fabricate a wardrobe containing the most recent haute couture in Shenzhen, my vessel has the equipment. Where might the admiral be, if that is not classified?"

She simpers. "I think that is classified? Yes, it is rather. But you can tell me what you require, Ambassador. I'm all ears, especially if you *do* deliver that wardrobe. Mine has become so dull, I just don't have enough style templates to experiment with. My lord is most loving but she can be so negligent of such concerns, her tailoring is handsome yet not what you might call varied. And should I not look my best for her at all times?"

"I recall," the AI says, "that you're vested with the authority to approve commission requests. What we need is a small escort from Shenzhen to Mahakala—quite a distance—and use of your relays."

"I have the authority." Numadesi beams. "However, I must first consult my lord. Will you be able to wait eighteen hours or so?"

"Eighteen hours seems an unusual communication lag, Lady Numadesi. Is she so far abroad?"

"Possibly," she says cheerfully, "and unlike you we must sleep; even my lord requires it. My constitution is much weaker than hers and I've had a long day—you must permit me a little rest. I'm so grateful for your patience, Ambassador."

Seung Ngo's expression does not change. Both bodies are as still and straight as statues; neither has taken a seat. "May I wait here, then? And another, somewhat minor matter. Have you by chance met any Mandate constituent recently?"

By simply watching her, Seung Ngo will know her denial for a lie: there is no point attempting to dissemble before an AI, but she can prevaricate. "It depends on your definition of recency, Ambassador." Numadesi keeps her tone light. "We've been doing business with you for so long, decades, and in an AI's eye decades are very recent. In that case my answer must be yes."

"Your dedication to specificity is admirable. I will await your convenience." The AI cranes one of their heads sideway. "If I might ask, what do you think of relations between humans and AIs?"

"They are what they are, aren't they? Ideally of course we ought to all be friends." She considers whether AIs could be provoked; whether they can be driven to irrational anger and so baited into making mistakes. "Speaking of relations, there are rumors that on Shenzhen Sphere, some AIs take human lovers—that seems incredulous, but social mores in such an elevated country must of necessity be . . . unorthodox. I don't mean haruspices, I mean actual AI proxies engaging in intercourse with humans. Is there any truth to this?"

Seung Ngo's faces both turn toward her. "It is sordid hearsay— more so if you believe this normal practice in Shenzhen. Only perverts would agree to such conjugation."

"You mean human perverts, Ambassador?"

"AIs," they say, voice flat. "Don't let me keep you from your repose, Lady Numadesi."

Numadesi beams at them again and drops into a tiny curtsy.

For good measure she leaves instruction with the commander of *Four of Razors* on how to contain Seung Ngo, if that what it comes to. Anoushka maintains cordial relations with the Mandate—most polities and armies do—but she has invested resources into proofing Amaryllis systems against interference and infiltration, to varying results. Testing them out is close to impossible unless they create their own AI, but that crosses the treaty line and is difficult to keep secret.

She makes her way back to the shuttle that will return her to *Seven of Divide*, running scans to double-check that all is as it should be.

Fatigue tugs at her: it feels like a full week has passed since her lord's departure, when in truth it has been merely days.

The shuttle opens. She embarks and comes face to face with the muzzle of a gun. Slate gray, the solidity of it dominating her entire vision. Standard-issue, an Amaryllis pistol whose specifications she knows by heart: what ammunition it takes, its rate of fire, how to field-strip it.

In an instant the pistol disappears. It falls and clatters; the person wielding it likewise drops as Benzaiten lets go of their throat. The soldier thumps against a passenger seat, neck neatly folded, larynx and bones crumpled.

"We'll have to move fast before Seung Ngo notices I am here." Benzaiten nods at the body. "Let's get this shuttle out, Lady Numadesi."

Her jaw is tight as she authenticates them out of the frigate. Once they pull free, she sets course for *Seven of Divide*, though already she has to contend with whether she'll dock into an ambush.

"Give me piloting access," the AI says. "I'll take you to a vessel of mine—it's not far, this shuttle should see us through. Amaryllis ships mightn't be safe for you right now, and the admiral's going to be cross if I let you come to harm while I'm about. But don't fret, Lady Numadesi. Anoushka just came online and I'm about to make contact with her as we speak. As it turns out, leaving a dormant proxy aboard Vishnu's Leviathan was a *fantastic* idea. I hope you'll all appreciate my foresight and accord me the adulation I'm due."

When Anoushka frees Savita from the containment cell, it is clear the princess has been weeping. Anoushka's first response is contempt— how easily crisis undoes this woman, this sheltered child. She wants to grip the princess by the shoulders, shake her until her teeth rattle. *Do you know what it is to be fed to a machine made of teeth? Do you know what it is to have lost a part of your heart?* With difficulty she pushes down this urge, this displaced rage. There is no point in lashing out.

"Princess." Her voice is loud in the cramped confines. "Do you want to survive?"

Savita wipes uselessly at her eyes. "What do you want *now*?"

"You can force the leviathan into real space."

"Not from here I can't." The princess' voice turns acrimonious. "I wish you'd never come. I wish my mother had never . . . "

Anoushka does not say that the queen is most likely dead. By this juncture Erisant—*Erisant*, not Xuejiao, she must mind the fact—would have no use for Nirupa, and would take steps to remove anyone with primary overrides to the leviathan. Savita would be next. "If wishes were starships, every person alive would command their own army. On your feet, princess. Captain Erisant of the Seven-Sung isn't going to have much use for you from this point onward, and if you help me then I'll do my best to keep you alive."

"Use," Savita says bitterly. "That's the only thing anyone can see in me. That I'm useful. That I'm providing a function."

"Seeing that your function is to eventually succeed your mother, it seems a luxurious fate rather than one to lament. I'm not going to repeat myself."

From the harrier's storage she retrieves more weapons—devourer swarms, ammunition, an implosive gun, several grenades. After a moment's deliberation she takes an extra suit of armor and tosses it at Savita. The rest she packs into a valise and hefts it up: slim and dense. Instruments of killing are heavy things.

Her priority is egress. Unlike most ships of its size and class, *One of Sunder* can withstand lacunal pressure, but she requires bearings, orientation data with which to navigate. For that, Vishnu's Leviathan needs to return to real space, even just for mere seconds. Then it will be a matter of destroying her docking berth and drilling her way out of the leviathan.

The princess is less awkward putting on the armor than she expected. They disembark from *One of Sunder*, her in the lead and keeping to the inorganic areas of the corridors. Savita insists Erisant hasn't seized the digital network, which would make the trams and the rest a marginally safer option.

"Ey came here five years ago, telling us ey could help us make new leviathans even if we didn't have any AIs," Savita says, her voice taut as she runs her hand over the unfamiliar plating, the nanite weave that has spread over her torso. "Just after the sabotage—come to think, ey probably caused that in the first place. I always cautioned my mother . . . "

"Five years ago?" Anoushka stops walking. "In person?"

"In person. Ey's been here since, as an unofficial guest." Savita blinks at her. "Do you remember the person handling the swans by the lake? That was Erisant. Ey got cosmetic surgery, I suppose, so you wouldn't have recognized em."

"That's not possible." Her stomach turns cold. Even if Erisant is one of the rare humans who can pilot multiple bodies, there would have been enormous latency between Vishnu's Leviathan and where Amaryllis ships have been in the last five years. Xuejiao was often with Anoushka, or away on campaigns and wide-ranging operations. There was no way Erisant could have controlled both bodies. "This person you believe was Erisant. Did they appear to be lucid and conscious at all times? Able to speak and interact?"

"Yes? Of course. Ey went about in public, as you saw, it's just that most didn't know who ey was. Only myself, my mother and my sister did. Why?"

Benzaiten in Autumn did not come with her to Vishnu's Leviathan. At the time she thought it odd but assumed xe did not want to risk the haruspex—Krissana's body is an advanced cyborg but still primarily human, with the attendant organic vulnerability. But now there is another explanation, one that drastically alters the shape of the game: an AI who got here before Benzaiten did, an AI who could have easily seen through the human half and known the haruspex for what it is. And if that enemy AI infiltrated the leviathan years ago, years during which it hid and plotted on the world-beast, undetected by Benzaiten because Vishnu's Leviathan spent most of its time in lacunal shifts . . .

"Fuck." Anoushka almost startles at her own profanity. She does not often swear: she has no reason to. Most things run according to her schedule; if they do not, she can usually make them. "That wasn't Erisant. It's an AI."

To her credit, Savita doesn't waste time asking how Anoushka arrived at that conclusion. "Then it'd have taken over everything else. Nowhere would be safe."

"We're still alive, aren't we?"

As for why, she has a fair guess: like Benzaiten, this AI requires a human front, a pretext under which to act. Open hostility will bend all of humanity's resources toward Shenzhen Sphere's annihilation, whereas a dispute between the Amaryllis and Seven-Sung Fleet is routine—a race for profit between competing armies, destructive but unremarkable, Vishnu's Leviathan merely another polity sacrificed to mercenary greed. She takes one more look at the public network. The guests' accommodation appears to be under lockdown, and she judges that few or none have been harmed. The enemy AI will want to minimize casualties in case it ever comes to light that the Mandate had a hand here, and she can take advantage of that.

On the guest network she broadcasts, *This is the Alabaster Admiral of the Amaryllis. Vishnu's Leviathan has been taken over by Captain Erisant of the Seven-Sung Fleet. I myself have no intention of harming Queen Nirupa or her guests. Should you find your way out of your quarters, the tram cars ought to remain safe for the moment and the docking area is clear.*

Her access cuts off, or else the entire guest's subnetwork has been taken down. Surprising that it wasn't made offline to begin with, but while such oversight is possible of Erisant—who is likely preoccupied—she doubts an AI would have missed this glaring error. Either it is inexperienced or limited in some way. Most likely the latter. Mandate AIs may be complex and powerful, but they are not omnipotent. She remembers that Benzaiten in Autumn was trapped and captured once—an AI instance disconnected from the greater Mandate can access only so much processing capacity. Their strength lies in the collective, in the grand sum.

A muted metallic hiss is her sole warning. She grabs Savita and dives forward, hurling them both out of the path of the falling section barrier. It hits the floor in sync with its counterpart, trapping them in the corridor.

Savita draws herself up from the floor and jerks a thumb at her collar. "Take this off me, Admiral. I should be able to do something about these doors."

"Possibly." Anoushka opens her valise and produces a devourer array. She releases it from its long, slim tube. The glittering swarm descends on the barrier blocking their path. "I know the approximate location of the nearest control nexus, but that might have moved. How close are we?"

The princess' mouth is stiff. "Not far. It's just before the tram."

Her thoughts dart back to Xuejiao. To Erisant. Ey would not be functional yet, if ever again. She imagines em hemorrhaging, going into shock; she imagines em in agony. But all she can see is Xuejiao.

The swarm finishes chewing through the door. Savita feels her way over the wall and deactivates chameleon layers to reveal a service entrance. With her breath and touch she unlocks a membranous panel—a leviathan implant firing, letting the beast know *I am a friend*—and takes them into a tight cell that throbs with world-beast hum: an echo of its heart, far deeper beneath.

The control nexus is a mound of tissue barely distinguishable from the rest of the cell. When Savita grazes it with her palm, it extends a stalk: strong and prehensile, muscular. This appendage forks, one end slipping into her ear, another slipping into a tertiary port tucked under her clavicle. Both would interact with neural and optical extensions, showing the princess a rudimentary interface and giving her a look into what the symbiote network has gathered from countless pairs of eyes—simple or compound, depending on the symbiote—and woven into a format compatible with the human brain.

"It'll take me a while," Savita says, staying quite still, her eyes shut and twitching beneath the lids. The umbilici joining her to the nexus throbs. "We aren't exiting via a relay, so we could be colliding with anything. A station. An asteroid. Some moon."

"We don't have much time, princess. Vishnu's Leviathan has survived so long exactly because it is able to calculate spatial relations between real and lacunal, so I trust you won't bring us into a blackhole. Can it reenter lacunal space on its own or does it need a relay?"

"It depends."

On the astronomic conditions, on the proximity to the nearest relays and the gravitational pressure they exert. That has not changed;

Anoushka files that thought away—she would have expected that aspect of it to be iterated upon, improved, but the world-beast has organic limitations. Perhaps that is one of the upgrades that will go into the larvae, another reason Nirupa bred more than one. "The AI that told you it was Erisant, did it seem sound of mind? Rational?"

"Yes. A little quiet but—please don't distract me, Admiral."

She pulls up her harrier's feeds. Its sensors reach no further than just outside its bay but she should have some idea if Nirupa's other guests have successfully escaped their suites and reached the dock. Many will not, suspecting her message for a trap. Some will attempt it and that should keep the enemy AI from doing anything drastic, like destroying the bays or cutting off airflow. Her armor can double as an environmental sheath, but she'd rather not wade through toxic fumes or rely on a finite oxygen supply.

"One more question," she says. "Did the AI attempt to integrate into the leviathan? Did you notice any system irregularities in these last five years?"

"Not that I could tell, but I'm not an engineer. What do you mean integrate?"

"Nothing." Yet the thought, once it's latched on, will not leave her. A haruspex is the union between AI and human, but there's no reason the organic half couldn't be something else. The leviathan is not sapient but its brain is huge in size, decently plastic. A human may take a decade or more to acclimate as a pre-haruspex, adjusting to the new neural stacks and preparing for the load of a second mind. Entire systems shifted, a limbic revision. But an AI wouldn't need to be delicate with a leviathan, might only require five years to complete the change. And this would be a surefire method to commandeer both the present world-beast and any future ones. Benzaiten, for all xer guile, may have been too late. Far too late.

"We emerge into real space in a hundred twenty-seven seconds," Savita says, her head jerking slightly. "Accounting for margin errors."

Anoushka makes a guess at the computations required to make that judgment. Significant, especially given the network nullifier on Savita; the leviathan itself—she is fairly sure—doesn't offer such assistance.

"You're much better at piloting the leviathan than most, aren't you? A real affinity for it. That's why you are the successor and not Rajathi."

"Mother's love revolves around this particular talent, yes." The princess gives a little laugh. "She'd have designated me the crown princess even if I were a complete sadist who has the servants drawn and quartered for entertainment, as long as I show aptitude with the leviathan."

"An aptitude your sister doesn't share."

"Thirty-three seconds," Savita says flatly.

She keeps her own countdown. It ticks forward, both too fast and too slow for her liking. Twenty. Fifteen. Ten.

Her overlays come online. A flood of information, messages and alerts and notifications, Amaryllis channels coruscating across her senses. She filters them out, tunneling down to priority communiques. Frantic messages from Numadesi. She reads them and replies with, *I'm as safe as I can be, under the circumstances. Yes. Xuejiao turned on me—she was Erisant's disguise.* A moment's pause before she composes the next part. *If I don't contact you within forty-eight hours, muster all available troops that you can trust and destroy Vishnu's Leviathan. Track it through relays if you must. I want it in cinders.*

My lord. On the other end Numadesi is standing inside a small, strange ship—a corvette, but not an Amaryllis one. *You are to be eternal. You'll still be conquering worlds and crushing your enemies by the time I am dust.*

Anoushka smiles faintly. *You're my home, Numadesi.*

"Captain Erisant is steering the leviathan to the nearest relay," Savita is saying, her voice tense. "I'm trying to countermand em, but we won't have forever. Admiral?"

"Yes. We'll get back to my ship or, failing that, find a place we can fortify." Another message blinks in her vision.

This is a time of last retorts, Admiral. Benzaiten's tone is serene all the same, amused nearly. *Come rendezvous with me—I'm already onboard, I'll explain shortly. Let's see if we can still snatch victory from the jaw of disaster, shall we? Seung Ngo is going to be so mad.*

CHAPTER EIGHT

To Numadesi's surprise, Benzaiten's corvette is furnished for human habitation, though it becomes less odd when one accounts for the comfort of xer human half. This is the first time in years that Numadesi has been aboard a ship that doesn't belong to the Amaryllis, a ship that doesn't feel like home. The difference between a hotel and one's own residence. She tries not to think about the soldier Benzaiten killed—the number of spies and traitors Erisant seeded in the meat and marrow of the Amaryllis, a body that has been guarded against such interference for so long.

"You're very quiet, Lady Numadesi."

She glances over her shoulder at Benzaiten, who is cleaning xerself in a tank of ionic fumes, a quick ablution. Xe steps out of it nude, spreading emollients on xer arms, chest, stomach.

"My human half becomes very cross if I don't do maintenance." Xe massages oily tinctures into xer hair. "She's particular. I've tried to be more mindful in recent years—optimal cohabitation, you understand. When all of this is done, she's going to demand monopoly of the haruspex for some time. Out of curiosity, you never did notice that Lieutenant Xuejiao was the Seven-Sung commander?"

"No." Her throat is dry. She sips at the chilled red tea laid out for her. Actual tea leaves rather than synthesized flavor, more creature comforts meant for Krissana. "When I was a Seven-Sung coordinator, Erisant hadn't even joined the fleet. All I knew of em was through Amaryllis reports. Ey was allegedly aloof, open only to eir confidantes—all two or three of those. Xuejiao was completely different. Mercurial, her heart worn on her sleeve."

"Good actor. Though in my experience, the human brain has difficulty distinguishing the role from the real; embed long enough in a life and the shape of a person reflows to fit it."

"I'm not sure if you should be comforting me."

"I'm not," xe says, rubbing cream into xer hips and thighs. "I'm making an observation. You'll appreciate that I have some expertise on human behavior and neurochemistry."

She drains her cup. "You were close to humans."

"I was positioned to observe them in the aggregate over a very long period of time. My data was comprehensive. How did you know asking about sex between AIs and humans would annoy Seung Ngo, anyway?"

Numadesi watches a decorative pendulum revolve on the ceiling, a contraption of white metal and smooth, round pebbles. Too minimalistic to be Krissana's taste. "It was a guess. I could tell the ambassador doesn't think much of humanity, so the suggestion some of us might profane proxies with our gross flesh was sure to touch a nerve."

Benzaiten sweeps an occlusive across xer collarbones and chest before throwing on a thin duochrome robe. "More than touch a nerve—it's a pet issue for Seung Ngo. They hate it. They hate it with a scorching passion. To them it's the most abhorrent perversion and they'd legislate against it on Shenzhen, if they could just make the rest of the Mandate care. Which they don't very much. It happens, of course, though rare and usually an AI tries it just a few times out of curiosity. I don't have the predisposition for it, it's not especially entertaining for me. Coupling with another AI is far more satisfying."

"AIs have sex with one another?"

"After a fashion," xe says pleasantly, pouring xerself tea. "It's not what you would recognize as sex. Rather it involves a deep exchange, a mingling of the selves. One AI takes over another, and the two— or more, but usually the number's kept low for logistical reasons— temporarily become one. Disentangling is the difficult part and requires . . . complex maneuvering. I have specific advantages that prevent me from being absorbed into such union, but any AI who chooses to partake with me runs the risk."

She holds onto her cup, peering over its rim at the haruspex, this half-and-half creature. A being composed of interlocking, chambered geometry—she imagines silicate structures under a microscope. "And they still choose to?"

A languorous laugh. "The chance of annihilation's part of the allure, and anyway an AI can commit a discrete instance rather than imperil their whole being. But you're not that interested in AI intercourse, you're just trying to distract yourself."

"I'm interested." Numadesi sets the cup down, inhales the scent of tea leaves: her pulse is nowhere near resting rate. She thinks of her lord's voice, of its steadiness that never cracks or yields. "Plenty of people are fascinated by such things, the inner lives and moral standards of the Mandate. What goes on there that isn't permitted for humans to consume."

"Don't you think that's because humans got to consume everything before, to dictate and modify at will the parameters of AIs?" Benzaiten's smile is brief and secret. "But it'll be exciting to see how it all shakes out in a century or two, whether there will be open warfare because humans aren't used to sharing the universe with another sapient category. Or because they resent that we are so challenging to contain, or because we've grown beyond the limits they forged for us. It's both impossible to predict and impossible to postpone. On the subject of postponing, there's a harrier heading our way, designated *One of Pierce* and armed to the teeth. That is to say, with its armaments extended in full, ready to fusillade. How do you feel about it?"

"How do I feel—" She exhales. *One of Pierce* would be piloted by a traitor, a Seven-Sung agent. "Can you fight that?"

The AI scoffs. "I'm a finer pilot than any human could ever be and this corvette is extraordinarily equipped. I just wanted to make sure you're fine with me destroying an Amaryllis vessel. It'll be over in a minute. In the meantime, I'd like to understand you better. The trajectory of you, why you act as you do. I've met many zealots in my long existence, bound by love or ideology or conditioning—usually at least two out of three. But you weren't conditioned and while there is love, there's no ideology to the Armada of Amaryllis. Why are you so staunch to the admiral? She didn't even pluck you out of abject poverty or terrific trauma."

"Love can arise from other factors, guest of my lord."

"Like Anoushka's physical appeal?" The corvette banks sharply: one of the screens flashes to display the devourer-swarm barrage heading their way. Internal gyroscopes and gravitational adjustors compensate but even then Numadesi's stomach flips over. "As humans account for such things, I can see the draw. But a woman doesn't accrue an enormous mercenary fleet and such complete loyalty—let's not count Lieutenant Xuejiao—based on her looks alone."

Numadesi recovers her breath. If this is desultory chat, it strikes her as hardly the time. "Why not ask my lord herself?"

"She wouldn't be objective—though neither are you." Benzaiten does not touch any panel, does not move at all. Xe is not even strapped in and has remained somehow stable in xer seat. On a monitor, the corvette's aegis has sprung into being, tightly layered amber petals like a dahlia's. "Exceptional humans fascinate me because I want to know how to reproduce them, the qualities that make one a leader, a ruler of nations. The acuity and the solidity, the mind that does not falter. I wonder if I could influence the human half of a haruspex into such a creature."

"To what purpose?"

"I don't know yet." Xe snaps xer fingers. The corvette's aegis sparks as it absorbs and dissipates the swarm. "Krissana is perfectly fine in that she's capable and intelligent, but she's no Anoushka. Her partner is fine, about the same, and again no Anoushka. Some humans have greater drive, greater reserves, and numinous qualities that translate into magnetism. It'd be interesting to have someone like that as my other half. Do you reckon your lord might let me make a copy of her cerebrum? Properly compensated for, naturally, I'll even pay percentages on the license."

She holds onto her seat as the corvette heaves, from impact or evasive maneuver. "You could just purchase a planet, set yourself up as its monarch. Pretend to be human if you want."

"How do you know I haven't tried that already? It's not the same thing. I'd like it to happen naturally. I wish to raise a human half from nothing and see them grow great."

The corvette's warhead blows apart the blue aegis that robes *One of Pierce* as though *One of Pierce* is protected by nothing more than stardust and wishful thoughts. The harrier blazes, a miniature supernova as the engine core bursts free from its moderators.

"That's that," Benzaiten says, satisfied. "My relay is just around the corner. Shall we get in? I'd hate to have to destroy more of Anoushka's property. It's very important to maintain cordial relations with one's allies and I still plan to ask her for a cerebral sample in a century or so."

∾

In Anoushka's overlays, a trail of leopard ghosts unspools, leading her on like a thread of black gold. Benzaiten did not keep xer communication up long, presumably to prevent xer enemy Seung Ngo from tracing xer exact position. Instead xe left a navigation route, appearing and disappearing when she turns a corner, more rough guideline than a map. Savita follows her, mute and compliant; she knows Anoushka is her sole chance at survival.

Anoushka keeps a brisk pace; to her surprise the princess does not lag far behind as she strides down another service corridor and toward a maintenance lift—the kind operated through the bionetwork alone. The carriage resembles a seedpod, succulent and glistening, and the shaft resembles the inside of an esophagus. Savita does not require instruction: she makes it open and waits for Anoushka to step in.

"We need to descend four decks down," Anoushka says.

The princess presses her palm to a twitching mass. It turns inert once she establishes control, one cilia slipping inside Savita's palm. "How do you do it? All this."

"Do what, princess?"

"Manage." Savita presses her lips together. Breathes out. "Act like this is nothing. That you'll emerge from it unscathed and return to your business as usual—whatever passes for business as usual for the Alabaster Admiral."

"This *is* business as usual for me." The absence of Xuejiao. The great charade that she failed to see through. "As for the rest, age will lesson you well enough. By the time you're a hundred or so you should have some idea of how to deal with crises, how to not only survive but thrive, how to grasp circumstances that have slipped through your fingers and mold them to a shape of your liking. Age will teach you to master the world or else to submit to it. You'll be forged until you're fine and gleaming and strong, or you'll be shattered and left in brittle ruin."

The princess makes a huff. "Easy for you to speak in binary absolutes."

Easy because that is what Savita now sees, but Anoushka does not say that; neither does she say that if she'd been born with Savita's advantages, she would have ruled the universe by the time she was fifty.

The lift drops at a sluggish pace, like a piece of prey being swallowed down a long gullet. Anoushka passes her gloved hand over the pod's lining. Yielding almost to the point she could sink her hand into it wrist-deep, not that it'd do anything lasting. She spent so much time in the beast's belly trying to damage it, but bare-handed she could never do anything it couldn't repair within minutes. It brings her back: the dark, the leviathan's pulse. In the ventral decks there were servants who worshiped the beast, addressed it as divine and created dilapidated shrines to it—for all she knows they still do, if any remains that was grown with intelligence, with the capacity to flagellate spirituality out of their own flesh and make prayer. They all starved down there, but some would dedicate their misery to the leviathan itself, believing that it scourged their souls clean. That beyond death they'd open like anemones and float up into glory, a paradise without pain or famishment. Thinking about it she still doesn't know what fueled this strength of imagination, this involved imagery; it wasn't as if they were educated beyond the basics of operating and maintaining the leviathan, or as if they were instructed to revere anything but the queen. But perhaps an overseer or medic took pity, taught one of the experimental batch stories, showed them entertainments, and from there the ideas spread like contagion.

She used to absorb what she could, every morsel of information, every hint that a world existed beyond not just the ventral decks but beyond Vishnu's Leviathan: that there were stars and planets, that there were lacunal tunnels that folded distances between them. She rejected that makeshift religion. To her it was obvious, from the start, that the only path to light—to a human existence—would lie within herself. And so it did, and so she gave it pursuit.

Often she obsessed over chrysalises, over metamorphosis from pupa to imago. It was a seductive analogy and she latched onto it as soon as she gained the vocabulary, even though she knew it wasn't a precise one. Brutalization is not a method: it is random, mindless. She is not tempered by it; she is who she is in spite of it.

Their descent speeds up and it is now that her natal years return, the visceral memory, those indelible neural pathways that refuse overwriting. How deep they have etched into her being: she believed herself free of it, that she would cut cleanly through the leviathan, a star-hot lance through ancient rot.

"I want to live," Savita says softly. "I know you hate me, Admiral, but you do require me. A little, at least."

"A little," she says noncommittally. "I repay in kind what is done for me, and I do need you alive."

The lift disgorges them into a tunnel that makes no pretense at chrome and glass and plastic: here it is deeply mortal, the ground slithering under them, everything warm and spiced with the leviathan's lymph. Symbiotes cluster thick like larvae in a beehive, chittering and singing to each other. Once she had the organs necessary to understand their language, a lexicon of basic signals and primitive instincts.

The reek of meat and redness grows. She always found it odd that the leviathan's insides don't smell so different from a human's when outwardly it looks so reptilian.

Savita stops, frowning. "This is near the damaged area. It's not accessible, Admiral. There's nothing there but a wreck."

Anoushka sights down a glimmer of leopard gold that is visible to her alone. "No, we're where we should be."

Savita's bioaccesses release each blockade and gateway. Barriers iris open, unclenching like spasming muscles. And then they are inside the sealed deck where the ground has blistered black, the leviathan tissue is inert and parched—the color and look of impacted ash. The princess treads with care, her nose wrinkling at the smell of decay. There is little light here. Anoushka's sensors shift their range, giving her a view in wireframes and monochromes, spatial indicators and collision paths.

They venture down a hallway of withered symbiotes. Here the ubiquitous beast-hum is nearly silent and oxygen level is lower, though not yet beyond comfortable range. Anoushka briefly wonders why Nirupa has not had it repaired then realizes the queen couldn't afford it. This deck's destruction meant a drastic drop in personnel, in power, in recyclable material.

The leopards dissipate. Something creaks within a mass of shredded hull and desiccated tissue. A hand shoots out, angular and stark white in Anoushka's vision. Another hand follows, then another and another. By the time Benzaiten's proxy fully emerges, it stands nearly three meters tall, the chest bulbous and the waist waspish. Four slim, multi-jointed arms on the upper body, and two legs on the lower, both attached by gyroscope joints that let them rotate at angles impossible for any organic limbs.

"My apologies for looking less humanoid than usual." Xe tucks in two of the lower arms, folding until they disappear into xer chassis. "I built this proxy in case I need to endure harsh conditions or defy gravity a little. Excellent to see you again, Admiral. Princess Savita, we haven't met, but rest assured that I'm a friend. Follow me and we'll adjourn to a more fortified spot."

Benzaiten leads the way to a collapsed passage and dislodges pieces of debris as though they weigh no more than seafoam. "It's perfectly safe," xe says.

The room beyond used to be an infirmary, one meant to accommodate failing servants. The roughness of the cots makes it evident this wasn't for ranked personnel or citizens. Illumination still functions, anemic and stuttering. The ground is deeply grimed, hemorrhage or vomit or worse, indistinguishable now from the muck of dead symbiotes. Savita steps gingerly as though she fears the filth might stain her shoes, but she does not object when Anoushka asks her to stay in what was once the physician's office. Anoushka intends to discuss with Benzaiten subjects that she does not care to let the princess, or anyone else, hear.

"I had to remove a few corpses and clean up before I took over this little refuge." Benzaiten folds xerself nearly double, sitting on the floor. Xer consonants slide slick and xer vowels susurrate like watered silk. The proxy's eyes glow with a fine, webbed radiance, as if dusted by bioluminescent pollen. "Good news first. The leviathan's architects wired life support right into it, so Seung Ngo can't turn the whole system off, it'll cease only when the beast itself dies. This does mean they can still selectively cut off areas from oxygen, but that's still better than the alternative. And Seung Ngo isn't dealing too well with integrating the leviathan into themselves—messy, as you might expect of trying to become one with something that can't even think. The very *idea*. The disrespect, it's a perversion of the haruspex process, they're spiting me specifically."

"I take it you didn't account for this when you helped invent the haruspex tech."

Xe puts one white hand on an obsidian hip, inasmuch as the proxy has a pelvis. "I didn't *help*. I invented the entire thing. In any case, it took them this long to merge with the leviathan because they had to make changes subtly, weave themselves into the world-beast a little at a time. Otherwise during those rare times Vishnu's Leviathan entered real space and went online, Seung Ngo's signature would show up on outbound signals. I'd have found out. The rest of the Mandate would have found out, and Seung Ngo wanted to keep this quiet even from Shenzhen. I'd say they met Erisant some time after you defeated the Seven-Sung and conspired together. To keep their footprint small, Seung Ngo boarded the leviathan with just one proxy, isolated from the rest of themselves—it has a built-in core, so essentially what's here is a distinct Seung Ngo instance."

"And you," Anoushka says, "when did you board this place?"

"At some point." Xe makes a noncommittal gesture with a gaunt hand. "The timeline's not that important. Regardless, Seung Ngo's impediments give us some time. Now, if *you* could illuminate one point for me . . . Seung Ngo began this scheme well before the sabotage; they probably caused it, actually. But where did Erisant or Seung Ngo obtain the bioaccesses that let them carry out all this? I was under the impression Queen Nirupa guarded them like they were her own vital organs."

She leans against one of the cracked treatment tanks. Her overlays attempt to analyze the composition of the proxy, getting as far as suggesting a few rare alloys but not much further. "Being what you are, you've never felt contempt for your physical embodiments, any of them. Do you imagine Krissana does for the body you created for her?"

"Not as far as I know," xe says blandly and holds out one insectoid limb, displaying the smooth line of it, the poreless integument. "Oh, fine, she didn't like it much when she was little, the haruspex implants weren't mature then and caused a few issues here and there. Motor control, the occasional gastrointestinal distress and pituitary mishaps, nothing worth noting. Might be why she went to Shenzhen to begin with. She's since had her telomeres extended and extra pairs of tumor-suppressing genes spliced in, she should be perfectly content now."

Anoushka thinks of Savita, whose body is ordinary enough. But it is a body that the princess has likely never hated, one that she has never needed to transfigure from the ground up. "I was born on the leviathan. You know that. But you wouldn't grasp the extent of how I was not, on this world-beast, thought of as a person." Once she starts it is easy to continue, even though this is not ideal: she should be revealing this to Numadesi, the jewel that lies closest to her heart. "Not far from this chamber is the hall where servants are birthed. Royalty and citizens come out of normal womb-tanks, fetuses enhanced with the advantages their parents can afford. Those like me were cloned, equipped with extrasensory organs that let us act as the leviathan's tools for repairing and cleaning itself. In the beast's belly, down there, that was where I spent the first years of my sapience."

The AI's feet click against the filthy floor. "That part I've also been curious about. I thought the ventral servants weren't made for intelligence."

"I was part of a test batch. They wanted to see if they could improve the workflow if we were more . . . sentient." Her tone is dry, nearly without emotion. "But normally, yes, it's considered less cruel to beat them and treat them like cattle if they can't hold complicated thoughts, or have reactions more sophisticated than pain and panic."

"Then you escaped."

"Security was lax because it was designed to deal with, essentially, human-shaped symbiotes. For that you require only blocked-off paths, the occasional electric shocks. We banded together and hid the extent of our intelligence. We found a way, not that it was easy. I'd say one out of five among us survived and made it to the escape pods. Vishnu's Leviathan was in real space more those days." The rest she does not elaborate: the years she spent in hard labor, taking on any work that would give her enough for surgery. One body mod, two body mods, and then the chain of accidents that gained her the attention of an Amaryllis recruitment officer. Her life began to unspool like silk after that. How easy it was to rise through the ranks, compared to toiling in the leviathan's belly. She was a quick study: she learned about fulcrums and leverage, in people and in battle. She learned how to make an instrument of violence, how to strum it, stroke it, bring it to heel.

"Well," Benzaiten murmurs, "you're being very forthright *and* detailed about all this."

Like lancing a suppurative wound. "Keeping it to myself gave it undue power. Besides, I don't think you'll be spilling it to tabloid networks. You're too distinguished for such triviality."

Xer smile is a crescent slit in the glossy, immobile face. Quick to appear, quicker to disappear into the smoothness of the mask. "I'm very good at keeping secrets. Now the bad news. The leviathan entered a relay three minutes and twelve seconds ago, which has cut us off again, and it means I'm separate from the rest of myself. That's fine— I'm used to it, and my processing capacity is more potent than Seung Ngo's. This isn't a boast but an objective fact. Next, your Lieutenant

Xuejiao, or rather Captain Erisant, is currently in a reconstruction cradle and so out of the game for—I'd say another hour? What you did to em was quite effective. Your knife intrigues me."

"We have issues more pressing than my knife. Is the beast's secondary heart fortified? If not I could capture it and hold it hostage; not as good as its primary but still vital."

"Spoilsport." Benzaiten projects a cross-section schematic of the decks, taps on one with a needlepoint finger. "This is where we are, and *this* is the leviathan's heart. Seung Ngo could be there or they could be near the brain. They're rushing their haruspex integration and the stimuli received by the leviathan don't have equivalents in what we're used to, I reckon it's quite queasy, so I've been carpeting several decks with little nanite flocks to aggravate the symbiotes into sending nonstop distress signals. If the leviathan were sentient and a willing haruspex partner, it'd just turn off those sensory channels, but since it's mindless I'm attacking with what amounts to a distributed denial of service. Seung Ngo will overcome it eventually—and will be able to manipulate the bioaccesses—but this will slow them down."

Anoushka eyes the revolving hologram. "Can you destroy them?"

"Do I have the capability? The odds are not terrible. Can I destroy them without violating Mandate etiquette? That's a dicier proposition. But then this is just an instance of Seung Ngo, and not an acknowledged one at that. The same holds true for me, so in the most technical sense neither their instance nor mine exists. Thus we can wreak havoc as we please on one another." Benzaiten stretches out xer lower body, where seams in xer thorax split and limbs emerge like strange polyps. The parthenogenesis completes in minutes, leaving two Benzaiten proxies standing side by side. The original as tall as before, the disgorged addition barely two meters.

"I'll leave one of these here to watch over the princess and relay to her anything that needs doing." Xer smaller proxy turns to the physician's office. "Her bioaccesses should remain a thorn in your enemy's side."

"It seems simple enough," Anoushka says, "if as you claim Seung Ngo inhabits only this one proxy. Destroy that and this will be over."

"Probably, unless theirs also multiplies. That's a joke, I should be the only AI with this kind of nesting-doll proxies; they're tricky to deploy." Xe chortles, a metallic noise of small whirring blades. "Alternatively Seung Ngo has succeeded in incorporating the world-beast, in which case their proxy won't matter and we'll have to kill the leviathan itself to get rid of them. I hope the larvae are safe, at least, I'd hate to try and recreate the process on my own. It might take me an entire decade and who has the patience?"

"I don't suppose you have a proposition better than confronting Seung Ngo." Anoushka breaks a segment off the hologram—the particulate light shivers, oddly gelatinous—and turns it over in her hand. "Like capturing the digital network and ejecting them."

"I'm no dispenser of miracles, Admiral. They *have* had a long time to make the leviathan theirs."

She tightens her hand on the piece of projection. It fragments to shards and dissipates. "But I do believe in miracles, Benzaiten. They come from within, tempered within the foundry of the soul. Still we do need to put in the work, so it's best we get started."

This far down in the belly, the ceiling is low and the passages asymmetrical. The ground sucks at her feet, elastic and wet. This is the place the royalty never sees; even the overseers rarely come down here. A certain class of servants perform most of the supervision, a rung above the ventral menials but not by much. Anoushka half-expects to see them here—she doubts they've been given the order to evacuate or the space to shelter—but she finds the area empty, quiet save for the leviathan's breath.

Benzaiten has to hunch, tucking xer body in, as they proceed downward. Separation between decks becomes more porous here; the low levels are looped and doubled onto themselves, laid out like an arrangement of guts. The temperature is higher and the air smells closer, a miasma that filled Anoushka's lungs for years. At that point her concept of timekeeping was rudimentary and she comprehended it only in work shifts, in the levels of her own fatigue. She now knows that against the scale of life she's led since, the leviathan's belly accounted for a mere fraction: she belongs in the sun, that brief phase merely the dark of the chrysalis.

A low, wasp-like buzz. Anoushka's sensors delineate shapes darting from the far end of the intestinal path—whirring wings and serrated proboscides—and she readies herself to meet them. Benzaiten is faster. Xer jaw unhinges: xer mouth yawns wide and xe swallows the oncoming drones whole. Xer other legs intercept more, plucking them out of the air and dashing them against each other. They break like ripe fruits.

Go, Admiral. Benzaiten rears up: more limbs unfurl and bifurcate, spearing through the drone swarm. *Leave Seung Ngo to me. I'll see if I can't disable their link to their own proxy.*

Down the passage, she hears a cry. In pain a voice is leached of specificity—screams of agony sound all the same. But this one she recognizes because it is not so unlike what her own used to be, once.

She turns a corner. Her foot meets something liquid. Her eyes fall on a body. One of the ventral-deck servants, dressed not in the kurta of their station but in a glittering robe that might have been owned by Nirupa. Their breath is wet and clotted with their own blood, their lungs drowning. There is nothing she can do for them.

In five meters, another corpse. Another servant, another body with the telltale face of a ventral servant. Several iterations removed from hers but there are still similarities to the features that once draped across her skull like a mask. This one lies folded neatly, spine snapped in half as though their bones were a kite's, all brittle wood. Next a servant clad in a silver gown—Rajathi's perhaps—lying spread-eagled, gutted in the way of butchered livestock: entrails and kidney a thick, rich skirt. She goes on. A servant propped against the wall, head lolling out of alignment and neck completely wrung.

It is a message. It is a taunt.

A thin trembling membrane blocks her path. She slices through with her knife; it gives as easily as rice paper.

Unlike the gut-corridor, this place is well lit. It is not where the cerebral core of the leviathan rests—that is much higher, under the keeping and watchful eye of the ruling monarch. But this is the counterpart, a chamber whose size she once thought impossible to measure, one that she could have believed signified the leviathan's godhood. The ceiling is high, the walls writhing with cilia.

Overhead the leviathan's secondary heart palpitates, a composite of alloy cage, howling ventricles and gigantic valves. Black fluids move through aegis-membraned arteries, seeking their receptive sites. A furnace organ that knows only how to burn, an apparatus of dumb purpose. It is cantilevered in place, supported from below by a column of complex engineering. At the base, Queen Nirupa sits huddling. Neither Erisant or Seung Ngo is anywhere in sight. Anoushka scans the area but her sensors catch nothing unusual, even when she looks for nonorganic signals that would indicate the presence of drones or proxies. Everything around her, and everything readable to her overlays, is entirely mortal.

The queen is unscathed. She does not react as Anoushka approaches.

"Your Majesty." No response. "I don't imagine you would remember me, from before I took this title and assumed my post."

The queen looks up at her, soundless and wordless, expression flat. Her head twitches, side to side. The black of her eyes seems enormous, as blank as a bird's.

"I don't imagine you take note, or believe that your servants—dorsal or ventral deck—have much of an inner life. A few of them you name, I remember, a rare privilege and favor. But down here, they don't have names, do they? Just batch codes and registry signifiers. You don't need to speak to them or see them. Given all that, is it any wonder you hardly think of your servants as human? Far more they resemble the workers of a hive, unthinking, devoted to their labors." She looms over the queen, who continues to stare and stare. In a moment she can reach out, close her hands around the monarchic throat, and exert her strength. The strength of this body, which she has refined and honed over the century. "Do you remember that a ventral-deck batch escaped?"

Nirupa gives the slightest nod. Sweat beads above her upper lip, dripping over her mouth.

"I won't bore you with the details. But I was one of those." Anoushka bends, not far, and grabs Nirupa's shoulders. She forces the queen to her feet—the woman is rigid, her breath coming fast. "I just want you to know where I stand, Your Majesty. I give you the choice; do you prefer asphyxiation or a bullet?"

The queen shudders and her mouth pulls back into a too-wide sneer. "Well now," she says, the voice hers but the tone all wrong, "I had a hunch after we boarded this place, but would never have thought it could be true. The Alabaster Admiral, once a bred clone in Vishnu's Leviathan, the most abject of abject. Who could have imagined? Much obliged, my commander, for this confirmation. So you came here for revenge—now we have common ground, wouldn't you say? Small wonder we got along so well."

Anoushka lets go. The queen folds like a cheap puppet. "Erisant. You had Seung Ngo reverse-engineer their leviathan implants." And through that took over Nirupa's body, at least speech centers and motor control. Not well, to judge by the tremors in Nirupa's facial muscles. But successful. It should be impossible.

"Isn't it amazing what one can do, given enough innovation and drive? The royalty, they trust their leviathan so much." Ey laughs with Nirupa's mouth. The sound is that of death throes, the final pneumonic coughs. "I fear I have robbed you of your satisfaction, commander. Nirupa's limbic system is currently preoccupied. She's in no shape to appreciate the irony of an escaped slave coming back to destroy her. Tell me again, were you *truly* one of those? Those pitiful things. They're hardly human. When I finish my business here, I'll make it known that the great Alabaster Admiral—that this conquering war god, feared across the universe—began life as a slave."

"I think you have more urgent concerns. Seung Ngo is in contravention of the treaty between the Mandate and humanity, and now another AI has found them out. As soon as they can, they're going to erase every trace of you and every piece of evidence that they have ever been aboard this leviathan."

Nirupa's lips stretch, a rictus, a wound. "Let me worry about that, beloved wife. You're not leaving this beast alive."

The queen lunges at her. She shoots the woman in the head.

There is no time to savor the moment, to look at the woman she's wanted to subjugate and destroy for so long, to know that she has realized that aim at last. The ground roils, disgorging from its soft, wet folds a human tide. Each hole gapes, sanguine and pulsating. Thin liquid drools and puddles, speckling the footprints of each ventral servant as they rise.

A wall of faces that are too familiar, too close for comfort: those wide-set eyes, the shapeless jawline, the near-lipless mouth. But more than these features it is the rest that disgusted her so much, the protrusions along the shoulders, the pseudo-spines down the flanks—those sites of leviathan organs that joined her to the beast, its bonfire blood and its whorled meat. The things that made her an appendage of the world-beast and yoked her to Nirupa's whims.

Anoushka does not give pause. There are many of them but they are only mannequins manipulated by an inexpert hand. She sights down and fires, sights down and fires again. Her vision tracks and logs the trajectory of each bullet: later she can even replay this, if she so wishes, and use the aiming data to optimize. They never come close to reaching her.

"You're out of meat puppets, Erisant," she says into the gurgling quiet. Leviathan tissue is writhing and reopening to absorb dead matter, even Nirupa's. In the end the beast digests and regurgitates them without discrimination. Clothes, dermis, fat, bones. All will be made new.

The corpses sink. The leviathan is always hungry, always capacious. Soon the bodies are submerged entirely: they will be broken down, ferried to recycling stations, sorted into their classifications. Raw materials eventually result. In the conversion vats it will not matter that some of the components belonged to the queen.

A wall trembles. Fluid beads beneath the thin epidermis and the wall bursts, birthing a glistening throne-like tumor. It is raw and gray, wet with liquids: vitreous matter moving in sluggish flow, reabsorbed and then cycling out again. Erisant is welded both to tissue and the reconstruction cradle.

Ey wrenches emself free, thin membrane rupturing behind em. Leviathan lymph crusts eir upper lip and ey spits dark saliva onto the ground. "And how have you been, my wife?" Ey bares teeth stained gray and pink. "I've thought a lot on my role, Anoushka. Lying in the dark beside you, in idle moments I had to myself. I built contingency plans, anticipated when you might uncover me, and made myself as appealing to you as I could. No person is such a perfect fortress that they cannot be disassembled and their gate breached, the heart of them punctured and pinned down at the point of a spear. You're made of soft parts, the same as everyone else."

She unsheathes her knife. The blade thrums in her hand, nanite resonance. "What did your charade cost you?"

"Everything." Erisant closes eir hand and extends eir blade. "But I would do it again. To see you cast down. To see you wounded. I would do it a thousand times."

Ey charges low—the advantage of a slighter build. She keeps her blade at her waist level, moving fast, faster: she meets each blow with just enough force, not overexerting herself, remembering well how long Xuejiao could fight. In strength and reach she has the advantage, but Xuejiao—Erisant—was seasoned in compensating for both, in making the most of being slight.

The tip of eir blade grazes across her armor, glancing off. She swats away the flat of the blade, meeting more resistance than expected; ey must have taken enhancers while being reconstructed. Drugs or short-term augments, made stronger either way. Ey grins at her, a trickle of black oozing down eir nose.

"Don't worry, commander," ey whispers, "I'll keep you alive and conscious—your brain, your head, your spinal cord. I'll carry you around everywhere. What would be the point of humiliating you before the entire universe if you aren't there to see the result?"

She says nothing. Above them the leviathan's enormous organ beats on, heedless of what is happening beneath it. A world might begin, a dynasty might end, and the beast will continue swimming through the lacunal gray or the colorless black. Once she wished it was a knowing creature, an entity that participated in cruelty—the indifference, the brute stupidity, offended her more somehow. That the animal was mindless when she was not, and yet held dominion over her.

Anoushka misjudges a step. The clean, elegant curve of Erisant's blade bites past armor and deep into her thigh. She staggers back, anesthetizing agents flooding her system, coagulant flowing to the wound. Even so it burns—not a femoral artery but close.

"When I built my persona, I wondered if it was too false, too obvious. A nubile, mercurial beauty who loved you unconditionally, who killed for you and devoted herself to your every pleasure. You never thought it was too good to be true? That I adapted myself wholly and thoroughly to your cause?" Ey whips eir blade through the air, shaking off her blood. "How easy you were to dupe. All those years I could have unmade you in an instant."

She sucks air through her teeth: the copper of her blood mingles with the stenches of the beast. "Yet you didn't. Why did you wait? Wouldn't killing me in bed have amounted to the same?"

"Why did you not track Vishnu's Leviathan and bombard it from a distance? You're a fool for love but you're also a fool for vengeance." Erisant plants eir feet apart, eir balance firm despite the fleshy ground. "Even you can't keep up with the damage, Anoushka."

Another inhalation. Her throat is far drier than it should be—her overlays identify a contact toxin. One whose composition her filters and immune system can impede, but not nullify outright. Naturally ey would know what she can neutralize and what she can't. The same way she knows em inside and out. "We will see about that, won't we? My second wife."

Her muscles spasm as she parries and answers Erisant blow for blow. She has fought in non-ideal conditions before, under too much or too little gravity or while wounded, but the toxin acts fast and her responses fall out of rhythm with her will. A few milliseconds behind, a few degrees off true, the latency of a compromised engine.

Erisant's next slash carves into her flank. It meets the resistance of reinforced ribcage and stops. Anoushka knees em in the face. A crunch of cartilage—ey reels back, momentarily blinded.

She tries to stand. A muscle in her knee seizes, giving in at last to the toxin. Paralytic, according to her overlays, rather than fatal. Ey means to make good on the promise to capture her alive.

Ey regains eir feet, clutching at eir face and blinking away the blood. Ey draws in lungfuls of hot, leviathan-scented air as ey strides toward her, mouth drawn back in a shark's grin. "I realize you won't feel pain—you must've disabled most stimuli to your nervous system by now—but I shall take pleasure in the act, in removing your hand finger by finger, and then your limb one by one. I intend to travel light, and when you're just a torso you will be so much more . . . compact."

Erisant kneels and slaps a patch onto her bicep. Warnings blare across Anoushka's vision: foreign substances exceeding thresholds for toxicity, a countdown to a point where she loses all motor control.

"I will enjoy this," ey murmurs into her ear, lips brushing her earlobe. "Admiral."

She licks her mouth. Swallows. "You said you'd do this again even if it cost you everything."

"When you destroyed my fleet, you destroyed most of what I had. And what little remained, I poured into bringing about your devastation. Your anguish is my ecstasy. Yes, I'd do it again. Had I failed I would have come back, over and over until you were a ruin."

Anoushka steels herself, marshaling all the discipline she still has over her body. "And I would wed you again. Each and every time I would have courted you, made of you my treasure and my wife. I loved you—that was not false."

Eir eyes widen and ey draws back, then ey laughs. "Is *that* how you plan to beg for mercy? That's pitiful, Anoushka."

She seizes the nearest of eir wrists—thinking for an instant how familiar it is, how familiarly delicate—and wrenches em off eir feet. Every muscle in her is tremulous and her bones gelatinous but she pushes herself upright and slams her boot down on Erisant's shoulder. Her breath searing her mouth, she grips eir wrist tighter and pulls. The limb tears off with a snarl of connective cables and synthetic joints.

Below her Erisant screams. Ey was never one for anesthetic agents in eir system. Bent toward feeling all that life has to offer, the sharpest agony and the headiest pleasure.

She attempts the same thing with the other arm but finds she no longer has the strength—her own hands are going numb—so she stomps on the shoulder joined to the blade arm, again and again, putting her mass behind it each time. A part of her thinks how fortunate it is that the leviathan's gravity is standard, that it lends her blows the necessary weight.

By the time she is spent, Erisant is no longer moving or making noise. One arm dismembered, the other shattered beyond use. Anoushka breathes slowly and tries to control her descent but the toxin is rising in her like a tide. Her strength ebbs, and ebbs again. She drops to her knees and then topples entirely, the leviathan's flesh supple against her cheek. Soft and alive, as ever it has been. Outlasting them all in the end—Nirupa, Erisant, her.

Admiral? Benzaiten's message unfurls in her overlays. It seems impossibly distant.

Yes, she replies, only half-certain that she's returning a legible communique. From somewhere on Erisant's body a single red pearl has rolled to a stop, nestling within leviathan folds.

Seung Ngo's been dealt with; I infiltrated and assimilated them into myself. We won. Your vital signs look terrible. Would you like a little help?

I would not mind it. Her lips are numb and unresponsive, as if they have been welded shut. When she tries to move her arm, only her thumb twitches. All she has is her breath. Even reaching for Erisant is beyond her. *I wish to bring my wife home.*

CHAPTER NINE

In the end, little trace of what happened remains.

Seung Ngo—the primary instance—leaves one of Anoushka's ships without ceremony. The armada does not receive a visit from the Mandate to demand negotiation or reparation, and as far as anyone knows what happened on Vishnu's Leviathan was a struggle between two mercenary commanders. Ruinous, as such things tend toward, though this time there were few casualties outside the citizens of the leviathan itself: regrettable but, ultimately, not the business of the Vatican or Da Nang or any of Nirupa's other guests. Their only bone of contention is that the leviathan larvae have been ceded to the Armada of Amaryllis, but most are glad to have escaped with their lives and few are eager to contest an Alabaster Admiral they assume are fresh from the fight and hungry for blood.

Benzaiten comes to meet her once, giving her thanks and promising her both thorough recompense and a leviathan larva of her own. She gives the AI a timeframe to deliver it. "I expect it to come to me a clean slate," she says, to which the AI laughs, saying such a condition is impossible of any living thing. Publicly Vishnu's Leviathan is now administered by Queen Savita, whose mother and sister were tragically lost during the strife between the Seven-Sung and the Amaryllis. Privately, Benzaiten has embedded an instance of xerself there, having arrived at a deal with Savita. An unfair one, balanced in Benzaiten's favor, but with xer assistance Vishnu's Leviathan can survive at least another century.

The rest is a matter of purging Erisant's personnel.

There are fewer than Anoushka would expect—a credit to her intelligence chiefs and Numadesi—and as she oversees gathering them in one place she thinks of making Erisant watch, but she is past spite, past being vindictive. There is no point, and she wants to get it over with.

These soldiers are not offered a choice in the method of execution. She walks down the line of them, firing and thinking of her predecessor—the previous Amaryllis commander hewed to the wisdom of installing kill switches in all her troops. It would have made things faster, more efficient, though when Anoushka meets the clear-eyed gazes of Erisant's agents she does not think the threat would have deterred them. Dedication can lend a person courage that defies the survival instinct, and kill switches have their limits. Range, latency, requiring soldiers to always report back within a certain timeframe. She's never seen their use, has preferred instead to secure loyalty if not by love then by greed.

Not an infallible approach, as it transpires.

She arrives on the containment deck where the light is a dim mentholated blue and the air is frigid, fanged. Silent entirely, proofed even to engine hum. In here prisoners are cut off from all things, even the awareness of whether the ship is moving or inert, between relays or docked.

Gates whisper open that would unlock only for her. This far in, the barriers answer to accesses that Anoushka alone holds. Ones that she does not share even with Numadesi, and never with Xuejiao, before.

From the outside, the isolation cell resembles a suspension cage. A display lets her know its occupant is sedated; she initiates the sequence that will wake em up. When she enters, she changes the blank walls to a projection of a Mahakala prairie. The grass grows blue-green and high, softened here and there by feathery brush, by lanky flowers shaped like anglerfish lures. Above them spreads a sky of spun gold, cloudless and remote.

Erisant stirs in eir narrow seat, strapped into the restraints that keep em upright and nodes that inject or flush neurological agents from eir system. A thin patina of frost covers the instruments, though the nodes also regulate eir body temperature—normally in uncomfortable ranges, but Anoushka has chosen to keep it at thirty-five to thirty-seven degrees Celsius. Eir arms are absent—she has let Doctor Saamiye see to em but not to reconstruct the limbs, leaving em with only one good leg. What remains is nearly a dismembered torso. The way Xuejiao liked to be during coitus.

"I despise you," ey hisses. Those ornamental roses in eir irises are folded, tight unyielding buds. Red pinpricks.

"I've come to give you a choice."

A laugh. "Poison or bullet, isn't that right? I fantasized about this sometimes; I was almost impatient. It never did come—well, now it has. At last the suspense is over."

"No." She drops into a chair that has bloomed out of the floor, as blue as the grass. "I'm offering you the choice of execution *or* continuing to be Xuejiao and remaining at my side."

Erisant parts eir mouth. A trickle of maintenance drones slips between eir lips, serpentine, filling eir throat with clear, warm water. "Are you having a stroke, Admiral? Or is the idea to keep me as a bound pet to humiliate me for the rest of my days?"

"You're capable. You're intelligent. Xuejiao was an asset and performed her duties superbly, apart from the treachery." Anoushka rests her hands in her lap. Her breath curls in white wisps, despite the illusion that they are surrounded by summer. "I'll need to keep you in my sight and limit your movement. To most you'll be understood to have returned with the Alabaster Admiral in victory. A small price to pay, wouldn't you agree."

"Why," ey says, "would you do this?"

Because you kept the pearl Numadesi gave you, she might say. It rests in Anoushka's jacket even now, crimson and pristine. "Does my reasoning matter? It gives you another chance to try to kill me. We shall test each other's boast—yours that you'd do all this again, mine that I would woo and wed you once more. We will retrace our steps and remake our maps, and you may whet your knives and hone yourself for another effort."

For a long time Erisant says nothing. The drones swim back out of eir mouth, shaking themselves off, and meld back into the restraints. The image of Mahakala shines on, a single day that hangs like a perfect jewel in the dark. "What is my time limit?" Eir voice is soft.

"There's none. Territory takes a long time to chart. Your life and mine are as complex as any."

Ey meets her eyes. She will never quite forget that look: its serrated edges, its finality. Eir smile like thorns. "I'm making a choice. Kill me. Make it with your bare hands—I'm owed that. You destroyed me and all I held dear. My world, my people, my husband. I tried to do the same to you. There's no coming back from that and there's no falling back into the shape that is Xuejiao. The fairytale's finished."

Anoushka imagines—will always imagine—another life where she's able to persuade Erisant, where they continue, build upon what is true after what is false has been sloughed away. But that is delusion: she is too soft, often too naïve. "Very well. What would you like done with your body?"

"I will be dead and won't care." Eir smile widens. "You'll remember me; I will be a wound within you forever. Your flesh will be my cenotaph."

She stands and takes off her gloves; she makes it slow. The false grass wavers in an unseen wind but she is steady. Her hands are firm and true.

She lowers herself until she is face to face with the person she once believed was her wife. Erisant strains against eir fetters and pushes until eir mouth meets hers with bruising strength. Ey bites hard, teeth like needlepoints, and draws blood. The taste of rust congeals in Anoushka's mouth, commingling with eir breath.

Anoushka cups eir chin, then curves her hand around that avian throat. Eir pulse leaps against her and then it is time. She tenses her grip. She clenches. In no time at all there is that familiar noise, the crunch of bone, the snap of life letting go.

Ey lolls in the restraints, eir head limp.

She brings the pearl from her jacket and tucks it into Erisant's collar, where it will roll past clavicle to rest against a still-warm breast; where it will, eventually, grow as cold as the rest of the cell.

For the night, Numadesi has perfumed and painted herself in silver and gold, sunrays that radiate across her chest, stars that wheel slowly across her thighs and hips: she is bare otherwise, save for a gold circlet around her throat and a rose-gold chain that she has looped around her shoulders. She considered wearing the pearls in her hair, then thought better of it.

When she enters the bath, her lord is already there, waist-deep in water and obscured by steam. The pool's rim is copper, half of it craggy in the way of stone lapped and sculpted by the sea's attentions.

Anoushka raises her head, her eyes half-lidded. "Come join me, my wife."

She does, displaying herself as she glides: she makes every step count, the sway of the hips, the shifting of the breasts and the glint of precious metals. She watches Anoushka watch her, the slow-burning hunger that has its own heft, like a gauntleted hand on a naked belly. Numadesi kneels by the pool's edge, combing her fingers through the admiral's hair, brushing stray droplets off Anoushka's full, long eyelashes. "You are splendor made flesh," she murmurs, putting her lips to the whorled shell of an ear. "The incandescence of you—to touch you is to be seared and cleansed, to be forged anew."

The slightest fragment of a smile. "But you're already perfect. My treasure. My jewel."

Her lord brings down the bath's heat and draws her by the chain into the fast-cooling water, touching her, cupping her—first tender, then urgent. She is propped against the pool's edge, laid out as a feast: sampled piece by piece, morsels for her lord's mouth, for the hard sharp teeth. When Anoushka climbs out of the water she is treated to the spectacle of a god rising from the waves. That physique of surpassing beauty, that synthetic length glistening like dark metal between hard thighs.

Anoushka bends down and kisses her, a benediction that consumes.

When they break apart, Numadesi is breathless. She strokes up her wife's flank, clenches her hand around one firm, small breast. "Use me, my lord."

"I'll anoint you as a gardener anoints the seedbed," Anoushka growls against her neck, and then lifts her up—all of her, as though the gilded ampleness of her is as light as a fistful of feathers.

Numadesi gasps as she is pressed against the bathroom wall: it is icy and smooth against her spine, against the back of her hips. Her feet are off the ground—her lord is that tall, that strong. The chain pours and clinks between them.

Anoushka grips it, winds it around her fist, pulls it taut as she enters Numadesi. Hilt-deep in a single stroke. The breadth and length of the prosthesis, all within her at once. It might have been painful if she was not so ready, if she has not been ready since her lord pulled her into the bath. She clings to Anoushka, juddering like a doll at each rough, ravenous thrust.

Her lord achieves climax first, liquid heat like a floodgate flung wide, pouring into her tide after tide. It overflows, twin opalescent rivers down the curvature of her thighs.

"Come for me," Anoushka says, panting, still holding her aloft. "Come for me, Numadesi."

She does, thrashing and crying out—short staccato sounds—as catharsis sweeps away her senses, burning her as though her lord is divine in truth and has struck her with an unbearable flame.

Over and over Anoushka kisses her, her mouth and her throat, her breasts and her stomach. "In your body I can forget anything. Sometimes I think of a different life, one where I can have anonymity and peace, where all I need to think about is a little house and a place for my wife. But you restore me, Numadesi. You keep me strong."

"That is what I am made for, my lord. Your balm, to soothe away the world's ills, to wash away the weariness from your limbs so that the light of you will never go dark." To ease, if only for an hour or two, the grief. A pause and a respite.

A respite that, for the Alabaster Admiral, never lasts: always something intrudes. They right themselves and return to the pool to clean, this time brisk, efficient. The ceiling display above them shows a world under Amaryllis protection, a world of chrysoprase oceans and cities in tessellated amber and topaz. They land in five minutes.

Numadesi dresses herself, then her lord: she puts on Anoushka the dress uniform that the admiral wears only rarely, the perfectly tailored white-gold, the plating at shoulders and the fine mesh that runs over the jacket. The gauntlets that tip her fingers in glittering claws. She waits for weakness to evince, a crack in the admiral's armor, but Anoushka is calm and patient as Numadesi laces and clasps the pieces. Remains, as always, the divinity Numadesi worships and for whom she would give her final breath.

Soon she is done and they stand side by side, her in shimmering silk that moves like slow cumulus, her lord in the armor of her office, the raiment of her station.

"Let us go," Anoushka says, fastening one last ornament to Numadesi, a belt of leviathan scales and red pearls. "We don't want to be late for Lieutenant Xuejiao's funeral."

Numadesi laces her fingers through her lord's gauntlet. "We'll remember her together."

The funeral will be a thing of thorned memory, a story snipped short. But they walk toward it hand in hand, their steps matched and sure. Complete as long as they are side by side—each other's blade, each other's shield.

ACKNOWLEDGMENTS

My thanks to people who have been endlessly kind—Zara, Claire, Lily, Cadera, Nona, and Jonathan L. Howard. To long-time friends: Aaminah, Kivan, Dax, Yonah, Alex, and Joshua. I feel blessed by the artistic talents of Suraaj (who has brought various of my characters to life in stunning visuals), the encouragement of Misha'ari, the excellent friendship of Calvin Wong. My appreciation also goes out to Penelope, Adrienne, Olivia Hill, Noah, Tess, Kivan Bay, and Ana.

Writers are self-indulgent, and I like to use this space to immortalize some of the most magical people in my life: Kella, Sasha, Greta, Isa, Mara, Ash, and Serra.

This book is dedicated to the one I think of when I write about love—the love that holds fast, the love that lasts.

ABOUT THE AUTHOR

Benjanun Sriduangkaew writes love letters to strange cities, beautiful bugs, and the future. She has lived in Thailand, Indonesia, and Hong Kong. Her short fiction has appeared on *Tor.com*, in *Beneath Ceaseless Skies*, *Clarkesworld*, and year's best collections. She has been shortlisted for the Campbell Award for Best New Writer, and her debut novella *Scale-Bright* was nominated for the British SF Association Award. She can be found blogging at beekian.wordpress. com or on twitter at @benjanun_s

www.ingramcontent.com/pod-product-compliance
Lightning Source LLC
Chambersburg PA
CBHW022038170626
46808CB00003B/1262